Time Will Tell

EDDIE UPNICK

Eloquent Books

Eloquent Books
An imprint of Strategic Book Group
P. O. Box 333
Durham, CT 06422
www.StrategicBookGroup.com

ISBN: 978-1-60911-097-0

Printed in the United States of America

Book Design: Judy Maenle

Cover Design: Owen William Weber

This book is dedicated to those rare individuals who risked everything to save the lives of countless strangers.

PROLOGUE

I made a promise to the man whose life story you are about to read. The individual who imparted his life's journey to me is now dead. The promise I made, and have kept, is that I would not release his story until at least ten years after his death.

To my mind, no greater man has ever walked our planet. If you choose to believe what you are about to read, I am confident you will come to the same conclusion.

Back then, I worked as a psychologist in a nursing home in Queens, New York. Actually, I shouldn't call it a nursing home; they prefer "adult living center" these days. After working there a few years, I wondered if I'd be doing that job for the rest of my life. At times, the prospect of that being my last job was quite depressing. The smells in the hallways, the complaints from our inmates (as I preferred to call them) and/or their children, all made me think about a career change. To maintain my sanity, I'd walk into the corridors, spot two people with walkers, and mentally bet which would make it down the hall first. I actually had win, place, and show betting in my mind.

Before you think me a monster, let me assure you I was not. I cared for these people, knew most of them fairly well, and conversed with them often. But, truth be told, my goodness, these places were depressing. Talking to old women about their fears of death was a daily occurrence for me. Most complaints were about the children who had put these people here. I felt most sorry, in a strange way, for those people who

1

had their minds intact. They knew what I knew about this place. I could go on, but I think everyone gets the picture.

One day everything changed. I was working behind a stack of papers in my office when in walked a man of ninety or so. I didn't see him enter, but he just stood there smiling until I finally did spot him.

I apologized for not noticing him, and he simply said, with a slight German accent, "Sometimes it's better to look busy than to be busy." I wasn't sure if he was razzing me or not, but I liked him right off the bat. He said his name was Jeff, and he wanted a room in my hotel.

"Why in the world would you want to live here?" I asked him.

"Because I'm old and tired and I have no place else to go."

I asked Jeff if he had Social Security to transfer to us for payment. Shockingly, he said no. Jeff told me he had no retirement pensions of any kind. I asked him how he intended to pay for his stay at the "Queens Hilton." To my surprise, he pulled out $90,000 in cash from a small bag he carried, and dumped it on my desk. As I looked up at Jeff with raised eyebrows, he said, "Will this cover me for a year or two?" Speechless, I just nodded yes. I did not work in admissions, but for this man, I decided to bridge that gap for him.

In the coming months, I became obsessed with Jeff's past. I tried several times, but could never pin him down into a conversation lasting more than a minute.

My poor wife had to listen to me ramble on about Jeff and how I needed to get to know him better. We had one small child and another on the way, so she had her own obligations to deal with, and little patience for me. "Just talk with him," my wife would say almost daily. Finally an idea occurred to me, after my wife said she was going to see her mom, and taking our child with her, for New Year's. My wife asked if I minded her being gone for New Year's Eve, and initially seemed angry at my enthusiasm when I told her she should go.

I knew this might be my chance to get to know more about Jeff. After Christmas I asked him if he wanted to spend New Year's Eve with me. When he said yes, I felt like I had won the lottery. That is how excited I was that he had accepted my invitation. In the brief conversations I had with him, Jeff had such a fascinating grasp of history and how the world seemed such a wondrous place. This air about him, that he knew something the rest of the world did not, subtly came through. I needed to know more, much more.

On New Year's Eve, I bought three bottles of Borolo, which cost me my week's paycheck. Honestly, I felt like I had a date with Angelina Jolie, only without the sexual overtones. My excitement level was incredible, as if I sensed something unusual was to be found out this evening.

I picked Jeff up from the adult center at nine p.m., then drove him to my house four miles away. After a few minutes of small talk we cracked open the first bottle of wine. I also had my tape recorder running, a note pad, and fresh coffee ready if needed.

Shortly after eleven, as the wine began to really take effect, Jeff looked me in the eye and asked my opinion of him. I told Jeff I thought he was the most mysterious and secretive man I had ever met.

Jeff looked at me for a moment, covered his eyes with his left hand, and asked me a simple question. "If I talk to you, will you promise never to reveal what I have told you until at least ten years after my death?" Before I could answer, Jeff's eyes turned to fire as he demanded my silence with a penetrating stare. I swore to him that I would not reveal anything he told me that night to anyone, until at least ten years after his death.

Now softening toward me, Jeff drank another swig of his Borolo, and smiled as he leaned back into his chair and ran his fingers through his still-thick grey hair. Much of what you are about to hear has been classified as top secret since before World War Two began. "Prepare yourself, young man, for a story that will shatter many of your known truths on Earth and even beyond." When Jeff said this, I got goose bumps all over my body.

CHAPTER 1

NAZI RULE

I was born in the year 2101, in Belgium. I was one of four leading scientists in the world working on the time travel experiments. The future I was born into was very different, hopefully, from the one your world will develop into. In my timeline, the Nazis controlled the world. Black men were used for manual labor, and indeed only a very few thousand Africans were left alive on the planet. The Asian races were all gone. Aryan purity ruled our day. Several thousand Jews were still alive, as some were able to conceal their identities from the Gestapo and the SS agents. The Arabs were all but gone, and their oil fields, or what was left of them, were safely in German hands.

"Shall I continue?" Jeff must have noticed my mouth was wide open as I listened to his opening monologue. I blurted out for him to continue, as I finished off the first bottle of wine and opened the second.

"Jeff, please tell me you are pulling my leg with what you're telling me." Jeff's eyes were very sad, as he simply, slowly, shook his head to say no.

The Fuehrer of our time was obsessed with meeting Adolph Hitler. The time travel project had gotten top priority. Funding was unlimited. Our Fuehrer wanted the project completed by the end of 2133, the 200th anniversary of when Hitler came to power. In my world, microphones were everywhere, as were cameras to follow all citizens' whereabouts. Informants were everywhere, you never knew who to trust.

I interrupted. "Are you saying that in the future, Nazis will take over the planet?"

"Hopefully not this future," was his reply.

In my timeline, Germany won World War Two. There were several reasons for this. Japan did not attack America at Pearl Harbor until November of 1942, delaying the United States' entry into the war. Germany was also able to defeat England before breaking their non-aggression pact with Russia, which gave Germany the luxury of never having to fight a two-front war, at least in the earlier years of the war. Many other smaller factors allowed Germany to develop atomic weapons first. V-2 rockets launched by land and later by submarines carried these A-bombs all over the globe; the Nazis eventually destroyed over 50 cities around the world to maintain total order and obedience to the Reich.

There were some limited successes. The Americans secretly developed the technology for weapons-grade uranium in 1951. They killed 20,000 German troops stationed in various locations within the United States with limited-range nuclear weapons. Four U.S. states were obliterated as punishment shortly thereafter. There truly was no free world left to speak of.

I was selected to join the time travel project because of my grades in mathematics and physics. On the surface I was a loyal Nazi, with few blemishes on my record. Hiding one's true feelings was a key to survival in my time. My wife and three children lived in a world I hated. No freedoms. They even had cameras in bathrooms. Thinking of those SS bastards watching my wife take a shower made my blood boil. Yet this was the world I was born into. If you had three years in a row without any marks against your loyalty record, one camera could be shut off in your bedroom for an hour a night.

In many ways the reality you are living in today is more technologically advanced than the one I grew up in 150 years from now. The Nazis feared any technology that could circumvent their spying abilities on the individual. Cellular telephone technology existed, but was only allowed by high-ranking party members. For the masses, the penalty for being found using one was death. The risk was simply too great. Informants were everywhere, looking to cash in by feeding information to the SS in exchange for money, advancement, or future favors.

The only small positive aspect of the society I was born into was that we had literally no crime in the world. No one ever had to lock their door or car. The SS had pass keys to everything, so they could enter anyone's home or place of business at their whim. The Nazis ruled with their finger on the nuclear bomb. It was the only way they could control countries half a world away from Berlin. In a way, we had the most capitalistic system on Earth, within the Fascist regime of course. The higher the office you attained and status in the hierarchy, the richer and more powerful you became.

I was introduced to the other members of the time travel team. It seemed I was the last piece of their puzzle. Victor Kartov was of Russian ancestry. The Nazis let him live only because he was brilliant and could help them further their cause. Kartov kept to himself most of the time, as we all did, fearful of any new person you would meet. Boris Kruger was Nazi through-and-through, always trying to steal your ideas and make them his own, kissing up to the SS guards, and being a very willing informant. Sigmund Lloyd was a gem of a man. His specialty was history. If we were successful in returning to the past, Sigmund would be the man to turn to.

Sigmund had long hair, a rarity in our timeline; he was an older man, with fatherly qualities. Finally, there was Mac, a free spirit everyone was afraid to get close to, because the SS watched him like a hawk. No one knew MacDonald's first name, so we just called him Mac.

The five of us worked together, day and night for over 9 years. The Fuehrer was pushing us hard to finish in time for the 2133 celebrations of the 200th anniversary of Hitler's coming to power. We were very close to completion. This is when things got interesting, and extremely dangerous for all of us.

One night, Mac came to my home for dinner, an unusual occurrence to be sure. I was always too afraid to speak with him at length, because the SS followed his actions so closely. However, Mac was brilliant and I was fascinated with his theories, so I invited him to my home. Before I had a chance to offer him a drink, Mac, without speaking, walked around, found all the hidden microphones in my home, and disabled them. Next, he proceeded to the living room where the main video camera was located. Mac disabled the camera in such a way that the goons watching wouldn't know anything had happened. Mac used a pulse-compensator, a device that took the last image shown and gradually modified it, leaving the impression it was a live feed and not old footage.

After all video and listening devices had been neutralized, Mac told me that the final component to the time device was ready for installation. Then he told me of their plan to go back in time and change history. I listened with great fascination and hope. Apparently, I was the last of the trusted four scientists on this project, excluding Boris of course, to be told of this plan. The dangers within this plan were enormous, yet Mac convinced me it had to be tried.

You must realize the incredible sacrifice each of us had to make. If we were successful, history would be changed and our own existence might be erased from time. If we were unsuccessful we would all be executed, and our families would probably be killed as well. The stakes were indeed high. I agreed to Mac's plan, but understandably wanted every detail thoroughly explained to me, and for this plan to be as fool-proof as possible.

Now came the really hard part for me: explaining this plan to my wife. I was sweating, nervous, speechless and scared to death. Other than these blood-pressure-raising issues, I was fine. The day after meeting Mac at my home, I met my wife for lunch and all those fearful feelings returned as I looked my beautiful wife in the eye over a tuna salad lunch. I gave my wife a special look she knew well. It was a signal to activate her sound-amplifying ear piece, something I had developed years earlier. In this way, we could speak to each other in whispered voices the SS microphones couldn't pick up.

After listening to the plan, my wife very calmly said, "You must do this!" She wanted our kids to grow up in a better world, as I did. To this day, however, I'm not sure she truly understood the ramifications of a successful mission: none of us might even exist. So many questions and so few answers. I gave my wife a special kiss the next morning as I left for work, kissed my boys and told them to obey their mother, and with a tear in my eye, I closed the door to this part of my life.

I took notice of everything around me that day, as if to make a memory for myself. Swastikas everywhere in sight, video cameras, SS men following people. Indeed, this was a world I was prepared to prevent, if possible. Mac had poisoned Boris the night before; not enough to kill him, but enough to make him call in sick. When I got to work everyone was tense; you could feel the anxiety in the air.

Mac had disabled all the listening devices and the SS guards weren't due to come into the lab for at least an hour, so we had time to discuss the plan. One other piece of news came to light at the beginning of this briefing. This was a one-way trip. Kartov had falsified some documents on the animals sent back through time and then brought forward again. The returning animals were all dead. But the autopsies showed that they were alive in the past, before being killed during the return trip. Kartov very cleverly kept this information from Boris, or the whole mission would have been scratched, or worse, for us.

Sigmund had determined our best hope was to return to 1938 and try to make some changes to the early years of World War Two. The rest of us really left everything up to Sigmund in this part of the plan. He was the most knowledge-able historian of our time. Mac's area of expertise was taking Sigmund's generalities and turning them into specific plans of attack. Kartov had secretly learned the Russian language at home in his spare time. Kartov knew he would be sent to Russia to try to get close to Stalin and convince him to break the non-aggression pact with Germany, and to help create a two-front war much sooner than it had occurred in our time-line. I had no idea what I was to do once we got back to 1938. All that I knew at the time was that Sigmund and I would be traveling together, which did put me at ease somewhat.

I commented that we needed to finalize exactly how we were to deal with the SS guards who would be in the lab with us. My nervousness increased when Mac gave me a flip answer that we'd drug them, or something. My nervousness at the lack of specifics in this approach was about to give me an anxiety attack.

Two hours later, we were ready to test the time device. Each of us carried a handheld computer able to recall any moment in history since Hitler took power in 1933. It was ironic, that because of the incredible detail the Nazis insisted upon to be historically accurate from the point that Hitler took power, that this attention to detail was to be our best weapon in stopping the Nazis in the past. We also had a currency-copying unit attached to this computer, able to copy any currency and counterfeit any denomination of paper money we encountered.

We all had identity papers dated for 1938. Our big problem was the two SS guards. Mac tried to drug them, but they didn't drink the beer we tried to give them. Mac looked at me in panic when they didn't drink the knockout potion. The guards were named Krull and Hillman. Krull was much younger, less intelligent but more sadistic. Hillman was trying to become head of the SS. He was forty years old and smart.

Kartov and Mac then resorted to that 20,000-year-old solution of hitting both men over the head with blunt instruments. We quickly set the self-destruct in the lab for three minutes, and then activated the machine and got inside the transport tubes.

CHAPTER 2
THE PLAN TO CHANGE HISTORY

We transported back to 1938, as planned. We materialized in a basement wine cellar in the same space that we occupied when we left. This was a time machine, not a space machine. What we did not know was that Hillman and Krull, though groggy, were able to escape the lab before it blew up. We were later to find out that apparently, Krull brushed the time circuit as they made their run into the time tubes, and the date changed from 1938 to 1937. Moments later, the lab exploded.

I suppose I could go into the intricacies of how the time portal worked, but trying to explain over nine years of failures before we stumbled upon the final formula may best be left for another time. Once we arrived in the wine cellar, we gathered ourselves and then tried to get our bearings. We took inventory of our possessions. Mac grabbed a bottle of a 1924 bottle of wine out of the wine rack and smiled widely, knowing that we had arrived in the past. Of course, none of us had any idea that Hillman and Krull returned into the past a year earlier than we had.

Sigmund's plan was rather straightforward. Victor Kartov was to travel to Russia and try to gain the confidence of Stalin's inner circle. Next Kartov would try to convince the Russians to pursue a massive arms buildup to prepare them for what was to come. Mac was off to England to try to use his knowledge of history and science to gain entry to MI-6. Eventually Mac's hope was to gain the trust of his superiors and break the German Enigma codes used to issue orders to the German commanders in the field. If England knew these plans at the same time the orders were issued, it would give the Allies a tremendous advantage. With our historical hand-held computers, Mac already had the codes broken, he just had to decide how best to impart these broken codes to his superiors. Mac did it piecemeal, so as not to draw suspicion. Mac told me later that he often found ways to give others in his department credit for the breaking of the codes.

I was lucky. Unlike my two friends undertaking their missions alone, I had the benefit of Sigmund's historical knowledge and companionship. Sigmund and I were headed to the United States to somehow find a way to talk to the American president and convince him of the imminent threat posed by Adolph Hitler, no small task to be sure. With our forged papers and the ability to create any other documents we needed, none of us had any trouble getting out of Germany. After hugs all around, we went our geographically separate ways, knowing full well that we might not see each other ever again.

On our boat ride to America I listened to Sigmund's theories, at times endlessly, about our best hopes to change the outcome of World War Two. It became clear that somehow, we had to find a way to get Japan to attack America sooner than they had done in our timeline. November 1942 was too late; Sigmund surmised that Japan's attack had to take place at least a year earlier. What an exciting time that was for us. Just thinking about what we were attempting to do gave us incredible energy and a confidence in our step. The fate of the free world's future depended on the four of us. It was an awesome responsibility, but at that time, we were up to the task.

As we passed the Statue of Liberty, we both teared up. Our history had the Statue of Liberty destroyed in 1945, but looking at her here in 1938 gave us even more confidence to make sure that that future would never happen. We arrived at Ellis Island and were passed through quickly. Sigmund had given us FBI documentation to speed up the process. We also had every other possible U.S. security agency documentation on our person as well, just in case we needed them. Our voice computer was an amazing device. We simply would say the name of the person we wanted to find and the date, and then the computer would tell us. This device was a key for us to succeed in our mission. Again, it gave us a great pleasure that the most sophisticated piece of future Nazi equipment was helping us stop them in the past.

We arrived in New York City with no luggage and only the clothes on our backs. We both realized that we had to get samples of the local currency so we could duplicate it. We needed to buy clothes and find a place to live. Our first task was to try to get a twenty-dollar bill to borrow so we could copy it into our scanner/duplicator device. Neither of us had any criminal talents at all, so for us, this was a problem. Sigmund and I both knew Mac would have thought of something in seconds, but we sat in the bar for five minutes staring at each other with blank looks on our faces. Moments later, a panhandler entered the establishment asking people for money. When this man arrived at our table, we asked him to sit down. We asked him if he had any money. The man began to get up because he thought we were panhandling from him, but we convinced him to sit back down.

We all just looked at each other for a moment, and then I asked him if he had a twenty-dollar bill on him. The man looked at me and said, "Who do you think I am, Rockefeller?"

Sigmund and I had no idea who he was talking about, so Sigmund went to his computer and typed in the name. "Oh, a millionaire of the twentieth century." Our vagrant friend was beginning to think he was in better shape than we were. He then took out a five-dollar bill, telling us it was the largest he had. Sigmund took the bill, put it into his scanner/copier and proceeded to print five hundred exact copies. The vagrant's eyes popped out of his head. I really thought Sigmund should have been more discreet.

The vagrant, who we found out was named Bill, asked us how we did that. I offered to give him twenty of these bills if he would forget what he had seen. He smiled and said, "I would have forgotten for much less." He grabbed his money and left quickly. We departed shortly thereafter, walking down the street until we saw a "For Rent" sign. We rented a room for the month and paid in advance. We were very lucky the landlord did not notice all the bills had the same serial number. Once in our room, Sigmund entered FDR's name and the date into the computer, and we found out he was in New York.

There was a Democratic fund-raiser at the Waldorf-Astoria Hotel. We showered and took a nap, then made our way to the hotel where the American president was speaking. I knew we were in trouble when I asked Sigmund what our plan was. Sigmund shrugged his shoulders and said, "We'll play it by ear." Now I was getting a bit nervous. But not nearly as nervous as I was after what the next hour had in store for us.

As we were walking down the street, Sigmund froze with a look of fear I'd never seen on his face before. When I turned to see what had frightened him so, it became all too evident. There was Krull in street clothes, ten yards in front of us. Before my brain had time to think, Krull walked right up to us, pointed a weapon through his overcoat pocket, and told us to move. He led us into a poorly lit bar, and we took a table in the back. My mind was spinning. How could Krull be here? Did the explosives not go off in the lab? Krull answered all our questions, and Sigmund and I didn't like any of the answers.

Krull explained what had happened in the lab, but there were many factors he did not know. One point in our favor was that Krull did not know there was no return trip possible for any of us. What Sigmund and I had not known was that Hillman and Krull had been here for a full year. Krull wanted us to return with him to Berlin and meet with Hillman; he felt Hillman would know what to do with us. I am usually not a quick thinker in these situations, but I said something that got Krull confused. I told Krull that our Fuehrer had asked us, privately, to come back and test the time-traveling device. I added the point that our Fuehrer didn't trust Hillman, which was why we tried to knock them out in the lab before we left. I'm not sure Krull believed us completely, but we certainly created some doubt in his mind.

Sigmund joined in when he saw that Krull seemed a bit confused. Sigmund told Krull, that our leader wanted us to try to kill the American president, which would quicken the Nazi victory in the war. Krull was now so confused, he ordered a drink from the waitress. We told Krull that we had to try to complete our mission as soon as possible. Remarkably, Krull eventually let us go. We assumed that he was able to find us using the Nazi tracking devices all citizens had implanted in their shoulders as children. This is why Krull had the confidence to let us go: he knew he could find us easily.

As we got up to leave, Krull took out the most hideous weapon of our century. Sigmund and I were terrified that he managed to bring it back with him. The weapon was called a Hydro-Eradicator. In an instant it removes all liquid from the body, leaving only chemical waste and bone fragments behind, plus the clothes those poor souls were wearing. We had seen many enemies of the state killed in this way. The fact that Krull had the weapon in this timeline was a very dangerous development. When we noticed the Eradicator Krull was carrying, we asked if Hillman had one as well. Krull simply said, "Of course."

We told Krull to meet us back in this same bar in one week. Krull agreed, and we left. As I retell this story, I still don't know why he let us go. Sigmund felt Krull enjoyed the chase more than the kill. At the time, we weren't sure if the Nazis of your time could find a way to reproduce these weapons or not. If they could, clearly, we might have made things worse. Much worse.

CHAPTER 3

CLEM RIZZOLI

Sigmund and I made our way to the Waldorf-Astoria Hotel. This is where I met Clem Rizzoli for the first time. This short, stocky man, who spoke with a heavy Brooklyn accent and needed to shave twice a day, was to become a great friend. Our first encounter, however, was not very friendly. Mr. Rizzoli was a trust-no-one type of person. His job was to protect the president, but he did much more than that. Clem was also a close adviser to President Roosevelt, mostly on matters of security.

Clem noticed us approaching long before we took note of him. He saw Sigmund and me walking down the street, looking confused and checking addresses as we approached the hotel. Clem and two men that worked for him approached us at the entrance to the Waldorf.

"Can I help you guys?" were the first words he uttered. When Clem heard our English, spoken with German accents, the hair on the back of his neck really stood up. As we hesitated to answer his initial question, Clem asked us forcefully to turn around and face a parked car. He then proceeded to frisk us. Clem found ID cards for every United States government agency with our pictures on all of them, and he found our handheld computers.

Clem then looked me right in the eye and said, "What gives?" His colloquial English was hard for us to understand, not to mention his later use of words like "fucking A," "dumbass," and "dickhead." Despite his strange use of words, I liked him. Despite our various ID cards, however, Clem still mistrusted us. Sigmund tried to explain, rather pathetically, why we wanted to meet the president, which Clem saw right through. "You'll see the president when the St. Louis Browns win the World Series," Clem said. Then, suddenly, Clem's attention turned to the president, who had just finished his speech and was returning to the limousine waiting in front of the hotel.

President Roosevelt was helped by a large man at his arm to walk out of the hotel entrance and down the steps towards the car. I felt it was now or never to make contact. I walked up to the president as Clem pulled his gun on me. I blurted out "We're Nazi defectors with urgent news about Hitler's war plans."

FDR gave us a quick once-over and asked Clem if we had been searched. We were ushered into the limo after Clem gave the president a positive nod. Our window of opportunity was now open.

FDR looked at us and said, "What war plans?" All of a sudden Sigmund just opened up. I suppose that his being an historian specializing in the twentieth century had something to do with his loquaciousness. He spoke faster than I ever heard him speak before. Without hesitation, Sigmund told FDR that Hitler was going to invade Poland. FDR did not act too surprised at this statement, but did ask us for proof. Sigmund went on that under the Versailles Treaty, Germany was only allowed to have 100,000 men in their army, that Hitler would discharge 100,000 men and then train another 100,000. Sigmund said that Hitler had over 3 million men already in his army and they were preparing for world war.

FDR was not surprised by these statements either. In fact the president jokingly said, "You must have been talking to

Churchill." At this point, Clem chimed in that we had security IDs for all of the major federal agencies. Clem was very impressed with the quality of what he called these fake IDs. Clem then handed our computer to Roosevelt to look at. FDR said, "This is a piece of extraordinary workmanship. How does it operate?" Sigmund began to show the president, but I pulled his arm back. Sigmund realized his zeal of the moment had to be toned down. We had to disseminate information slowly. This was not the time to share future technology and all of our secrets.

We were taken to Washington for further debriefings. Since we had been hesitant to show the president how the handheld computer operated, we temporarily lost a bit of our standing with Clem and the other gentlemen in the room who were trying to extract information from us. Sigmund then released a piece of information that sent half the men running from the debriefing room.

Sigmund told Clem "Hitler is working on an atomic bomb that could destroy entire cities with one blast."

I then asked, "Could we speak with your leading scientists to discuss this matter with them?" We were not granted an audience with scientists from the United States for some time. I suppose your government wanted to know more about us before granting such a request.

Shortly thereafter we were allowed to leave, as we had little proof to show the American authorities of our accusations. We were followed, however. When we got back, the two men in trench coats and Stetson hats, who had followed us on the train to New York, were hard to miss. The back of our right shoulders was where the transponders that Krull used to find us were located. We made a mental note to try to have the transponders in our shoulders removed when we had the chance.

Sigmund and I were actually happy to be followed by the American agents, as Krull was to meet us shortly. If we were lucky, perhaps the American agents would arrest Krull. I also feared Krull might use his Eradicator to kill the men following us. If possible, I would not let that happen.

Krull was waiting for us in the bar that we had met him in a week earlier. Coming right to the point, he asked, "Why didn't you kill the American president as planned? Unless of course you were never going to do it in the first place. I tracked you to Washington DC and I know you had opportunity, so explain."

Perhaps we felt safer because the American agents were outside the bar watching us, but whatever the reason, I told Krull to be patient. "First we have to find out their weaknesses and exploit them." Krull smiled, took off a black glove, and commented that we were beginning to think like SS men. Suddenly, Krull noticed the two American agents looking through the window at our table.

Krull began to take his Hydro-Eradicator from his pocket, telling us, "You seem to have been followed by American intelligence. I will take care of them" As Krull began to stand up I grabbed his arm to stop him, but Krull brushed me aside, and seemed as anxious as one of your Western gunfighters to face off with the Americans.

Sigmund and I signaled to the agents outside that the man who came to meet us was dangerous, but they didn't seem to understand our gestures. Sigmund and I both got up from the table and walked outside. We got there in time to see Krull pull his Eradicator from his pocket and gesture for the agents to walk into the nearby alley. Sigmund and I were unarmed, so our options to help these American agents were limited, especially after Krull noticed us walking behind him. Krull, still believing that we were on his side, asked us to keep an eye out on the entrance to the alley to make sure no one else was watching.

One of the American agents shook his leg, and a gun fell to the ground as he kept walking. Fortunately Krull did not notice. Krull ordered both men to turn and face him. Before I could pick up the gun and aim it, Krull fired on one of the agents, leaving nothing but clothes and chemicals behind. I will never forget the horrified look on the second agent's face as Krull turned the Eradicator towards him. I fired the gun three times, killing Krull before he could fire the Eradicator again. The American agent thanked us, picked up the Eradicator, got on his walkie-talkie and requested assistance. Moments later, four more men arrived to pick up the remains of their man and bag Krull.

This was the evening I really got to know Clem Rizzoli. Clem came alone to our apartment with a thousand questions. Clem wanted to know exactly how the Eradicator worked. When we told him that it removes all the liquid from living things, he turned white. I wanted to tell him everything but couldn't, at least not yet. Sigmund and I decided to tell Clem the Eradicator was a German prototype weapon, and there were only two of them in existence. We also told Mr. Rizzoli Krull was an SS agent sent to kill President Roosevelt. After we said this, Clem said to us in classic Brooklynese, "You fucking guys are giving me a headache the size of Detroit. Don't go nowhere."

CHAPTER 4

MAC MEETS CHURCHILL

Meanwhile, let me fill you in on what Mac was doing in England. I'm piecing this together from what Mac told me years later. After he made it successfully to England, throwing up violently in the English Channel on the way there, he went directly to #10 Downing Street. Mac, despite having the historical computer in hand, thought Winston Churchill was the English prime minister at this time. Of course he was not; it was Neville Chamberlain. Two armed guards stationed outside the prime minister's residence asked Mac what he was doing. Mac said he wanted to meet Winston Churchill. The guards laughed and said, "He hasn't got the job yet. If you want to speak with him, check the pub two blocks away."

Mac found his way to the pub and spotted Churchill sitting alone at a small table. As Mac made his way to the table, two MI-6 agents at the bar got up and grabbed Mac before he got to Churchill. Churchill took momentary pity on Mac, who I suppose didn't look too threatening at the time. The agents frisked Mac, finding his computer and then his MI-6 security card. One of the agents handed the security ID card to Churchill. Churchill said to Mac, "I thought I knew most of my officers in MI-6?"

Mac said he just stared at Churchill and said nothing for thirty seconds or so. Churchill, with that dry sense of humor of his, said, "I had no idea I was so good looking." Mac was in the presence of the key to English history, and quite probably any chance at an Allied victory. Churchill signaled away the two guards to return to the bar, so he could speak briefly with Mac. "You have my ear, young man, what's on your mind?"

After his initial shock of seeing Churchill, Mac regrouped his thoughts and came right out with his mission. He told Churchill he wanted to work in the cipher division and signals school in Bletchley Park. Churchill seemed confused, as Mac had already shown his MI-6 identity papers. Mac then told Churchill his papers were forged. Churchill signaled to one of the agents at the bar to come over. Mac thought that he was going to be arrested, for impersonating an officer of MI-6. Churchill just wanted to compare his man's ID card to Mac's. Churchill was impressed with the forgery.

As Winston got up to leave, he told his MI-6 man to put this young man to work in Bletchley Park at once. "We need as many resourceful young men as we can find these days." What Mac did not tell Churchill was that MI-6 had been horribly infiltrated by Nazi sleeper agents. Mac knew that his first job was to expose these men, and quickly. In our timeline, Churchill died in 1940 at the hand of one of these sleeper agents. Mac had to prevent this from happening, at all costs.

Mac already knew the names of all German sleeper agents in England; he just had to find a way to discredit them or have them killed. Mac had to round up these sleeper agents quickly, before they scattered under their own fears of being caught. This was not going to be easy. Mac had to find a high-level person he could trust, then convince this person all these people he was to name were indeed German agents. Mac said he spent the first two weeks just looking around the offices for a high-level person he could confide in. Mac's main problem was that in those first weeks, no one really knew or trusted him. Like all of us, he spoke English with a

German accent which, to use your baseball expression, put two strikes against us.

Mac never found that person to trust. He thought about telling Churchill, but didn't think Churchill knew him well enough to believe him either. He had to think of another way. As fate would have it, one of the German agents from Mac's list inspired a new way Mac could discredit and kill these German spies in MI-6.

Mac was invited to dinner by one of the German spies on his list. Mac accepted the invitation, and decided to convince the German spies on his list that he was indeed one of them. Mac spent several days meeting all the various agents in different locations, trying to gain their trust. He spoke perfect German, had knowledge of the future Nazi offensive, and he carried that Aryan arrogance when he was with these men. Gradually, they became sure he was one of them.

Each of the Nazi sleeper agents in MI-6 was given only the names of two other fellow agents, so if they were caught, only three could be arrested. Mac had nineteen men and women on his list. By knowing the names of all nineteen people, he was able to convince them that he was sent from Berlin with new orders. The Nazis were brilliant in the professions they had chosen for the nineteen sleeper agents. Seven worked in MI-5 or MI-6 directly. Four were women working as secretaries to high-level English officials. The others were businessmen selling faulty munitions to the British, and high-level factory workers ready to sabotage the British war machine when called to do so.

Mac asked one of the munitions experts to build a bomb capable of destroying a large room. When the bomb was ready two weeks later, Mac said he was going to lure Churchill into a trap and blow up the room. Of course, Mac's real plan was to kill as many of these nineteen German agents as possible.

25

Mac planted the bomb in the basement of an abandoned store, and rigged a timer with a thirty minute countdown. After asking all nineteen agents to this room for what he described as new orders from the Fuehrer, he knew he was committed to this plan of his.

The meeting began at 7 p.m.; the bomb was due to go off at 7:30. When I asked Mac how he got out of the room after setting the timer, he said he told the group that he had to go to the bathroom. Mac fled the building and the bomb went off shortly thereafter. Mac had killed eighteen of the nineteen German Agents, but the one who had survived was the most senior member of the MI-6 group of spies. The surviving German agent accused Mac of setting the bomb, and Mac was arrested by English intelligence. Mac wasn't sure what he should do at this point. If he didn't defend himself with proof of some kind (which meant using his computer to show that he was from the future), he would be executed for murder and treason.

Mac asked to see Churchill, though he doubted he would come. This whole bombing incident was kept from the public, at least at first. Churchill did come to see Mac, but he came with the German MI-6 agent who escaped the blast, and was Mac's accuser. After the German agent tried to further convince Churchill of Mac's guilt, with Mac offering no response to these accusations, Churchill asked to talk to Mac alone. Once the German agent had left the cell, Mac decided to tell Churchill everything. Mac needed his computer to have any chance of convincing Churchill that he was a time traveler sent to stop Hitler.

Churchill told a guard to get Mac his handheld device, at this point humoring Mac more than believing him. Mac later told me that Churchill was so angry that he threatened to strangle Mac himself for killing all these people. Clearly,

Mac had a lot of work in front of him. When we planned this trip back in time, we had not anticipated telling anyone from this time period who we were. Well, all plans go off course sooner or later. Mac was to be the first one of us to describe our mission to anyone from this timeline. The question was, would Churchill believe him?

Mac said he took out his computer and handed it to Churchill. He asked Churchill to type his own name in the device. Churchill reluctantly complied, then turned white as he heard aloud what the computer said, "Winston Churchill was shot and killed on December 4, 1940 by Wilfred Brewer, a German agent working at MI-6." As fate would have it, Wilfred Brewer was the survivor of the blast and Mac's main accuser. Churchill was not completely convinced; he thought Mac invented this story to clear himself. Further proof was needed. Mac then asked Winston for the exact date. Churchill found it strange that Mac didn't know what day it was, but complied. Mac then typed in the computer asking about the precise date that Hitler was ceded Czechoslovakia, an appeasement move led by Neville Chamberlain. The date was two days hence. The computer voice said, "German forces marched into Czechoslovakia unopposed with England and France showing no teeth for war." As Churchill listened, he realized that Mac was probably telling the truth and that he was possibly not from this time.

Mac felt that this was his best chance to convince Churchill whose side he was really on. "Mr. Churchill, this handheld device you are holding is a future historical account of this war. I am one of four scientists who have returned from the future to try to change the outcome of this war. Our mission is to make sure Germany loses this war. Billions of lives are at stake. There were nineteen German agents work-ing in London that had to be eliminated to assist in this altered result. The last one is my accuser, who would shortly be your assassin. If you free me, I will help England break all the German Enigma codes and do everything I can to make sure we win this war."

Churchill looked Mac in the eye, and at least partially believed him. Churchill ordered the German agent, Mac's accuser, into the cell with them. Churchill then asked Mac to turn the computer voice on. Mac typed in the German agent's name. The computer voice then told of the German agent's mission and ultimate goal of killing Churchill. The German agent panicked and tried to escape, and was shot by the guards outside the cell. Churchill asked Mac not to speak of "this time-travel business" to anyone else. Churchill was not totally convinced that Mac was a time traveler; however, he couldn't explain this futuristic handheld computer that spoke, nor what this computer said about the now-dead nineteen agents. Churchill had Mac watched closely, but he clearly trusted him to a point.

CHAPTER 5

DEMONSTRATING THE ERADICATOR FOR ROOSEVELT

Now, back to our situation in the United States. Clem Rizzoli asked us to a meeting in the war room in the White House. Clem was holding the Eradicator in his hand, kind of playing with it. I asked him to please put it down on the table. Clem realized what he was doing, and complied with my request. Clem turned to me and said, "You know, the president wants to see how this thing works. He's on his way down here." Sigmund and I just looked at each other, as the president entered the room. The president asked us how the weapon worked, and how many of them there were. Sigmund took the lead at this point.

Sigmund thought there was a chance Roosevelt might declare war with Germany on the spot, if he could convince the president of Hitler's full intentions. Sigmund told President Roosevelt, "The weapon is called a Hydro-Eradicator. It removes all liquid from the body of any living thing." The president looked skeptical until Clem chimed in what was left of the American agent, nothing but clothes, chemicals, and bone fragments. Roosevelt asked us for a demonstration: he had to see this with his own eyes.

A large rat was brought into the room. In front of military men and the president of the United States, Clem handed me

itor and I "eradicated" that creature. As the experi-
d, four of the men in the room grabbed their papers
and left. The president asked us how many of these weapons
existed. I told him there were only two, both prototypes.
FDR seemed relieved to hear that. We told the president we
believed the other weapon was in Germany.

Clem Rizzoli slid a picture in front of me and asked if we
could identify everyone in this picture. The picture was taken
in Berlin, of Hitler, Speer and Hillman. Seeing Hillman with
Hitler was frightening. When I showed the picture to Sigmund,
he had a similar reaction. I told Clem and the president that the
picture was taken of Hitler, his close friend Speer, and Alfred
Hillman, a high-ranking member of the SS. Clem seemed
relieved, because no one else in the room knew who Hillman
was. I told the president that in our opinion it was Hillman
who possessed the last Eradicator weapon prototype.

I suddenly became brave, and asked President Roosevelt
to let us return to Germany and try to find a way to get the
other Eradicator away from Hillman. After a few hours of discussion, the president agreed to let us go. I asked the president
a long-shot question, if we could take the Eradicator with us,
but he logically refused our request. Clem and the president
both knew that if we were captured, the Allies couldn't afford
to have both Eradicators in German hands.

Sigmund and I also knew the Americans wanted to reverse-
engineer the Eradicator to try to find out what made it work.
We hadn't realized it at the time, but the Eradicators were made
from never-before-seen elements found in a meteorite that
landed in Russia in 2078. Duplicating the technology would
be impossible. I was certain the Germans of this time period
were also attempting to duplicate the weapon and would surely
fail, unless this rare element could be found inside an existing
meteorite somewhere on Earth.

Within weeks, Sigmund and I were on our way to London to meet with Mac, which we were really looking forward to. On the trip across the Atlantic, we pondered many things, including Kartov's fate, and anything else we could do to help change the outcome of this war. We would get to meet Victor Kartov again, briefly, but not for some time. As the boat pulled into port, Sigmund commented that this war could go either way, with the fate of the free world at stake. No pressure.

As we disembarked from the boat, word came through that Hitler had invaded Poland. The war had officially begun. Sigmund and I were brought into a top-secret British command headquarters. I remember a large war board with moving pieces showing Nazi troop movements into Poland, tanks, troops, everything British intelligence had found out. That is where we spotted Mac, dressed in uniform at his cryptology station, looking oh-so-British. When we all made eye contact, we raced at each other and embraced. I'm certain that the rest of the British officers in that room felt our actions strange, as this sort of hugging was not a British trademark. Mac told us that he was in charge of breaking the German Enigma codes (which he already had broken). Mac whispered that the British thought him a defector, and that was why he was having such success breaking codes.

CHAPTER 6

SIGMUND AND I
MEET CHURCHILL

Mac told me he had to tell Churchill everything, just to get out of a firing squad. That piece of news threw us for a loop. We then told Mac that we had met with the American president and gained his confidence. Before Mac began to smile about that piece of news, we told him that Hillman and Krull had returned to the past. Mac thought this an awful development, so we gave him more bad news, that they brought Eradicator weapons with them. Mac exclaimed, "Wow, you guys are full of horror stories!" Mac got tapped on the shoulder; Winston Churchill was ready for us downstairs. As we made our way into the basement of this facility, Mac asked us to be honest with Churchill. After Mac told us that he had told Churchill everything, we figured the cat was out of the bag, so we'd be totally honest with him.

What a thrill to meet Mr. Churchill! After the briefest of introductions, he started asking questions. We were sure he would ask us about time traveling, but he bypassed those questions for the moment. Churchill wanted to know what it would take to get America into this war. Sigmund explained that America had an isolationist movement led by Charles Lindbergh, and that President Roosevelt would not consider joining the war until after the election in 1940, at the earliest. Sigmund went on to say FDR wanted to help Britain, but needed an incident of some kind to get Congress behind any war aid. Then our conversation moved to Hillman with his Eradicator, joining Hitler's inner circle. Mac was very concerned about this, but Sigmund was not. Sigmund felt Hillman might be used to help the Allied cause. He wasn't sure how, but he did turn out to be right.

Churchill was scared. He knew that Russia and/or America had to join the fight, and soon, or all might be lost. I told Churchill I would try to get to Hillman, gain his confidence somehow, and attempt to get Russia to break the non-aggression pact with Germany. I had no idea how to do any of those things, but felt Churchill needed to hear me say it.

Mac came up with a general plan, and then Churchill spoke with FDR to firm it up. Mac simply said that Germany or Japan had to attack an American possession, and that would give America cause at home to help England. Churchill then told us that he would be assuming the role of Prime Minister, and Neville Chamberlain would be stepping down. After we congratulated Churchill, Sigmund said that history had recorded Chamberlain as the fool for trusting Hitler, with his famous "Peace in our Time" speech. But, Churchill calmly stated, "Neville Chamberlain played the fool to buy more time for England to prepare for war. It would be best noted in your history books in that way."

Sigmund made note of it, as he was politely slapped down by Churchill. Winston made himself a drink and offered each of us one, which we refused. Churchill casually stated that he estimated the Americans could produce 6,000 planes and tanks per month, if they entered the war effort. Churchill then said, almost to himself, "We'll have to hold on until America exhausts all their reasons not to go to war." Churchill was pleased that he was the only person in this timeline that knew of our true origins. The fact that FDR hadn't been told everything, and Churchill had, put a large smile on his round face.

Before Sigmund and I left England for the European mainland, we did manage to help the RAF perfect an advanced radar system, which gave the English the ability to see German planes approaching from a greater distance. Mac and I just tweaked their existing and quite workable system to give it a bit longer range, in their detection grid. The English Spitfires could fly at a higher altitude than the German bombers, so with the radar detection, it was relatively easy for the pilots of the Spitfires to fly higher and get behind the bombers. This created great success for England during the Battle of Britain, which was to come.

At this point, Sigmund threw me a real curveball. Sigmund said he wasn't going to Berlin with me; he wanted to find Field Marshal Erwin Rommel. I thought this a terrible idea, but Sigmund felt that Rommel might be able to deter Hitler's coming death camps, due to his renowned social conscience. Sigmund went on that, from his accounts of history, Rommel hated the Nazi atrocities, and that somehow Rommel would be able to talk Hitler out of them. I tried to postpone Sigmund's plan at least until we were able to get the Eradicator away from Hillman. Sigmund was quite determined, and somewhat pig-headed about this. I couldn't stop him.

Now I felt alone as never before. I was on my own for the first time, and honestly, I had no plan at that moment. My thoughts were with Hillman and what effect his arrival might have made to the outcome of this war. As smart as Hillman was, he wasn't an historian, so he truly was a random element in this equation. Would he help or hurt the Nazi cause? Only time would tell. As I made my way into Germany, the sights I saw were particularly unnerving: Jews, Gypsies, and the ill being herded into cattle cars as they embarked on their one-way trips to hell. I think I was more angered by watching the beginning of this cancer take hold than seeing it in my own timeline.

Sigmund was correct about something before we split up. He felt that Hillman might have orders for his Gestapo and SS people to watch for two men of our description traveling together, so splitting up may have been the safer plan. We had no way of knowing if Krull had gotten word to Hillman that he found us in New York. I made my way into Rotterdam by small boat from England and then to Hamburg, mostly by train. Once in Hamburg, I sat down at an outdoor café to have lunch. As I was minding my own business, a beautiful woman asked if she could sit down and join me. I said yes.

CHAPTER 7

LOUISE

Her name was Louise, and what a beauty she was. She was blonde, blue-eyed, large-breasted, red-lipsticked, and your typical Aryan goddess. Louise then scared the daylights out of me. She pulled a picture from her pocketbook, looked at it, and then asked, "Are you one of four scientists who traveled together?" I thought for sure she was an SS agent sent by Hillman. I saw no reason to deny what she already knew, so I said, "Yes, I am."

Louise had a great sense of humor. She must have seen how scared I looked. "Relax," she calmly said. "I'm here to praise Caesar, not to slay him." Now I knew she was sent by Mac. Mac used that expression so often during the nine years we worked together, none of us could bear to hear it. However, I was thrilled to hear that line now.

Louise was a top British agent working in Germany. I had assumed she was bringing me some sort of information, but as it turned out, her orders were to help me in any way she could. I asked Louise how she found me. She laughed and said, "I guess you aren't very observant, are you?" She went on to say that she had followed me after the boat landed in Rotterdam, and on the train to Hamburg. As I began to apologize, she cut me off and asked me to follow her. Louise wasn't comfortable in such a public place. I followed her back to the hotel she had just checked into.

Louise and I spoke for hours, mostly about the best way we could get the Hydro-Eradicator away from Hillman. In my timeline, the Eradicator was called a V-33, but most users of the weapon preferred to call it the Eradicator. None of our ideas for getting our hands on the weapon seemed truly feasible. When I told Louise that Sigmund had headed south looking for Rommel, she was as shocked by what Sigmund was attempting to do as I was. She didn't give Sigmund much of a chance to convince Rommel to confront Hitler over his "social policies." Of course she was right. It was getting dark, so we ventured out for dinner. I felt that Louise was under my complete protection due to the perfect identity cards I carried with me, which made me a colonel in the SS.

Before we finished dinner, Louise must have noticed that I had been staring at her cleavage all night, because she just smiled, grabbed my hand and led me out of the restaurant. When we got back to her hotel room, she asked me if I needed anything.

"A cold shower," was my reply.

As she slowly began to walk to the bathroom she said, "I thought scientists used all of their energies mentally."

"Not all," was my fading reply. With that, I still do not know if it was the crush that I had on Louise, or the strict interpretation of her orders, but she gave me the best night of physical passion I had ever experienced. No slight to my wife in the future, but with those damn cameras on us at all times, it was difficult to perform this sort of task at optimum levels.

When I awoke the next morning, more relaxed than at any time in my life, Louise managed to make some coffee and bring it to me in bed, with only a thin robe draped open on her body. I learned something that morning. I queried Louise, "I hope we can repeat this again some time."

She smiled and said, "We'll see." I was reminded of an expression I once heard: Women needed a reason to have sex, while men just needed a place. Apparently, it wasn't my wit and good looks, just her orders "to take care of my needs," that gave me this incredible night.

Anyway, the problem that I had when discussing our plans was that I didn't know how much Mac had told Louise. I was fairly certain our true origins were not known, yet how far was I supposed to go to help Louise fill in the blanks about us? Mac and I both knew Churchill wasn't going to tell anyone about us, with the possible exception of the American president. It was at this point that I had discussed Hillman and the secret weapon he had in his possession. Louise knew that we had to try to get this weapon back at all costs, even it were to mean our lives.

Louise asked me how the Eradicator worked. I told her the clear plastic gun fired a thin beam of very destructive light. I did not explain the gruesome effects, however. Louise was also extremely curious about my handheld computer and how it operated. I toyed with the idea of running Louise's name through it. Then I thought to myself, what if the computer tells me she dies tomorrow? I argued with myself that since my arrival in the past her future had been altered, so it didn't matter what the computer said. The only thing I was certain of was that thinking about time travel alterations gave me a migraine headache.

While in the bathroom, I did put Louise's name in the unit, and there was no record of her. This told me that she probably survived the war, changed her name and assimilated into Nazi society. I had no doubt she could lead the underground movement if she were so inclined. It didn't take me long to realize that Louise was a born leader. Two days later, Louise got word that Sigmund had been detained for questioning by the

SS, no doubt because he had tried to contact Rommel and the SS wanted to know why. After our debriefings in the United States, I figured Sigmund could come up with some answers for the SS that might help him obtain his release.

After thinking about Sigmund's being held for questioning some more, I began to get much more nervous. Even after I heard he had been released, I assumed that he had been followed. Perhaps Hillman was using Sigmund as bait to find the rest of us. I was certain Sigmund knew he would be followed, so I guessed he would not try to find me. I later found out he tried a second time to see Rommel, which no doubt created Nazi suspicion of Rommel himself. I also wondered if Hillman had with him a tracking device that carried the frequencies of our shoulder-implanted transponders.

The German people were euphoric at this time. The blitzkrieg of Poland had been more successful than anyone could have imagined. That Aryan feeling of invincibility was becoming stronger by the day amongst the German people. The cancer of Nazism had surely taken hold quickly in Germany. The German military, the SS and Gestapo were not the only Germans to blame here. Even the average German citizen got caught up in Hitler's perverted vision of Aryan superiority. Though I was born in Belgium, it still made me ashamed to be German.

I used my computer to give Louise a perfect copy of an SS lieutenant's papers. Of course, I had made myself a colonel. Louise really began to question who *I* was after she saw how easily my device printed these false documents. Yet she managed to keep quiet for the time being. Louise and I had an easy time traveling about, now that we both had papers. After all, we spoke perfect German; we walked with Aryan confidence in our steps, and strode confidently arm-in-arm. Yes, we were a happy Nazi couple out for a stroll. As we lunched that day, Louise had come up with the most logical plan of action. Louise suggested that we make our way to Berlin and follow Hillman. If he carried the Eradicator on his person, we would use Louise to lure him into a trap and somehow take it from him. I agreed to the plan, and we made our way to Berlin. We successfully followed Hillman without his knowledge, but never saw him carrying the weapon. By then the Battle of Britain had begun, and the German Luftwaffe was taking quite a beating. Hitler wanted answers. Add this to the news that dozens of German agents in England had been killed or captured, and Hitler must have been fuming. This is when Louise made a suggestion that was our best chance to sabotage the German war effort from within, but it was also the most dangerous plan for me.

CHAPTER 8
MEETING HILLMAN AGAIN

Louise's plan was simple. I was to walk up to Hillman while he was eating breakfast and report what I had accomplished to help Germany win the war more quickly. Louise reasoned that Hillman would have me watched closely, but would give me access to the German advanced weapons program because, with the losses at the Battle of Britain and Hitler's being on the war path, Hillman would want all the help he could find to give Hitler some good news. Once I agreed to Louise's plan, she looked at me dryly and said, "This plan might work, or Hillman might shoot you on sight."

To me, the hardest part of this simple plan was the first two minutes. Could I convince Hillman that we hit him over the head in the lab because the Fuehrer of our time did not trust him completely, and wanted the scientists alone to test the time device? I doubted I could convince him totally, but all I needed was to create a 20 percent doubt in his mind to keep myself from being shot. As I made that walk across the street towards Hillman, I wasn't sure if I'd make it to the other side. Hillman made eye contact with me, perhaps when I was fifty feet from him. He then removed his Luger from his holster, but didn't point it at me. He simply held it.

My heart raced as I stood five feet from him. Hillman stared for a moment, then said, "Am I to assume that you are giving yourself up?"

I stared quizzically at Hillman and repeated his question. "Give myself up? I have been looking for you. I have much to report to our Fuehrer."

Hillman asked, "Which Fuehrer?"

"Actually, both," I replied.

Now Hillman crinkled his eyebrows; I had him curious. Louise was right: playing to Hillman's ego was indeed the best course of action. I spent hours telling him one untruth after another, trying desperately to gain his confidence. When I offered to work on building new weapons for Hitler, though, that sparked his interest.

Hillman walked me back to Reich headquarters. I walked in front of him, of course, as he kept his hand on his weapon. While we made this walk Hillman told me something that was great news to the Allied cause. Hillman bragged that he had convinced Hitler to break the non-aggression pact with Russia. He egged Hitler on, saying it was Germany's destiny to rule the world, so why wait? Hillman had advanced the timeline for a two-front war, which was great news for Britain. To this day, Hillman may have done the most to change the course of the war by convincing Hitler to attack Russia sooner than he had done in my timeline.

Hillman's lack of historical knowledge regarding the sequences and events of World War Two could clearly work in our favor. Maybe it was because of what Hillman had just told me, but suddenly I had a quicker pace to my step. Meanwhile, Mac had broken all the German Enigma codes, so Churchill got orders the German high command was issuing at the same time the German officers in the field would get them. When France was under attack, for example, England wanted to help the French more, but Britain had to prepare for an attack as well. However, after a decoded message revealed there was not going to be any imminent attack on England, help was made available to the French.

I kept telling myself that if I were successful in gaining Hillman's trust, there would be great opportunity to feed false information to the German high command through him. It was far easier for a civilized man to act like a Fascist Nazi, than for the reverse to be true. With Louise's help, I knew I could do it. Louise's role would be to meet me outdoors somewhere, so I could speak to her covertly once I gained Hillman's trust.

Once inside German command headquarters, I noticed a man reading a German newspaper which read that FDR had been reelected. I believe the date was November 6, 1940. Roosevelt had told us that he couldn't truly help England until after his election to a third term. Now that he had accomplished this task, we felt help would surely come. It was only days later, that German agents discovered a "lend-lease" plan FDR and Churchill had worked out. America was to send fifty destroyers to Churchill. On paper it was a "loan," but in reality it was how America could help Britain without a declaration of war.

The German high command was divided as to what to do about America at this point. Their three choices were to ignore the fact that the Americans had just given England fifty destroyers, to declare war on America, or to just sink as many convoys of American supply ships crossing the North Atlantic as possible.

They chose the third option. German U-boats had a field day sinking American shipping. The worst was yet to come for the American ships, as Germany had just launched their "unsinkable" battleship *Bismarck*, whose sole purpose was to patrol the North Atlantic and sink any and all Allied shipping.

Meanwhile, Hillman put me to work in his lab; my job was to reproduce as many Eradicator weapons as possible. I told Hillman, "The Eradicators were created using as-yet-unknown elements from a meteorite that had crashed in Siberia in 2078." Hillman barely batted an eye. Opening a file cabinet drawer, he removed a small piece of rock, which he said was from a meteorite that crashed in North Africa in 1938. Before I had a chance to respond, in walked Sigmund wearing handcuffs, with two SS guards at his side. Hillman ordered his guards to remove the handcuffs. We were honored guests.

Hillman turned to Sigmund and asked why he kept trying to see Rommel. Sigmund calmly stated something about being a big fan of the greatest German general of all time, and a once-in-a-lifetime opportunity for an historian. He laid it on pretty thick. Hillman ignored Sigmund and then surprised us by inviting us to his lavish residence. He had already stolen a few paintings from French museums and put them on his walls. Apparently Hillman and the head of the Luftwaffe, Herman Goering, were competing for the most looted paintings to hang in their homes.

Over a large dinner table, Hillman calmly stated, "I haven't heard from Krull in some time. Would either of you happen to know his whereabouts?" We both looked at each other for a moment and shrugged our shoulders. "You both realize, of course, Krull contacted me when he found you both in New York City. He said you were going to kill Roosevelt. Why didn't you?"

I blurted out, "The opportunity never presented itself." Again, Hillman more or less ignored the answer to his question. After giving us a tour of his beautiful home, Hillman told us he had no intention of going back to our time. Sigmund and I were relieved, since that option wasn't possible anyway.

Hillman then walked us downstairs to his game room. Hitting a billiard ball or two, he asked us, "What was your true intent in coming back to this time? Were you going to try to change history, or were you simply trying to escape to the past where a better life awaited you?"

This time it was my turn to ignore Hillman's question. "You've done pretty well for yourself in this time. Do you also get to drop the gas pellets in the concentration camps?"

Hillman stared at me. "You see, Doctor, you've given your true feelings away here. Actually, with the Eradicator we can kill these people in a much more civilized way, don't you think? Stop thinking in twentieth-century terms."

Sigmund spoke up. "You are going to kill ten million Jews, with just one Eradicator?"

"Funny," Hillman responded, "that is exactly the question that Hitler had posed to me. I will come to the point, gentlemen: if you two help me build more Eradicators, I will let you live and perhaps even enjoy the spoils of a quicker Nazi victory. If you don't help me . . . well, then, what possible use would you be to me?"

Hillman's attempt to scare us fell short. In my opinion over ten million Jews would be killed in this war, not the six million widely reported. The numbers in Russia and the Ukraine were vastly understated.

I told Hillman the most sophisticated equipment available in this time would be required to properly examine the meteorite.

Hillman thought all meteorites had the same elements in them. Clearly, he did not have a scientist's mind. Sigmund was in the dark on this, but played along with me. I was buying time. We ended up telling Hillman that we needed more of the meteorite to finish the job, to see if we could build more Eradicator weapons.

He turned to Sigmund and said, "Pack your bag; you are going to meet your idol after all." Sigmund was being sent to North Africa where the meteorite landed. It was a few miles outside of Tobruk, which was fully under Rommel's control at that time. So far, Hillman seemed to be helping our cause.

I was glad Louise had talked me into leaving my handheld computer with her, but Sigmund had his taken from him by Hillman. So Hillman had access to new information about the past he did not have before. This was a most negative development. I kept Hillman at bay with a concocted story of needing more of the meteorite to produce any weapons.

Now things got a little interesting. Hitler was pressuring Hillman for results, so to deflect attention away from himself, Hillman asked me to lunch in Berchtesgarten with Hitler.

CHAPTER 9
MY LUNCH WITH ADOLPH

How cozy: just the three of us for lunch, with the beautiful Bavarian Alps all around us. Hitler was just being dropped off in his staff car, and as he approached, I saw the fear in Hillman's eyes. I was anxious to meet Hitler, so I could see for myself what type of man he really was. That did not take long. Two young blonde waitresses wearing dirndls were extremely attentive. Strangely, lunch was half over before Hitler said anything to us. This I will never forget. With food still in Hitler's mouth he said, "The Eradicator works on Jews, but what about Communists?"

That one sentence told me all I needed to know about Adolph Hitler. Even Hillman was initially embarrassed by the question, and then he answered, "Mein Fuehrer, the weapon works on all living things, even Communists."

Hitler laughed as food dripped from his chin. "Good news, Hillman, good news."

Hillman then introduced me to Hitler, and told him I was the scientist who would make thousands of Eradicators for Germany. Hitler glanced at me, but did not make eye contact. "This is good, very good. Keep up the good work."

Then Hillman made a tactical mistake, and I loved it. Hillman told Hitler, "If anyone can make more Eradicators, it is this scientist." He pointed to me.

Hitler lost his temper and violently threw down his napkin. "If?! There are no ifs, Hillman. When I tell you to do something, you do it! There are no if's, is that clear?!" It was such a pleasure to watch Hillman squirm in his seat while Hitler screamed at him. Hitler was impossible to please. If you had good news, he wanted better news. If you had bad news, that is where the expression "kill the messenger" began.

I then risked offering my opinion on the war to Hitler. I felt this might be my only chance to try to influence him. We had to get Japan to attack America sooner in this timeline. I spoke confidently when I said, "Mein Fuehrer, why don't you convince Japan to attack America as soon as possible? After all, they gave Britain fifty destroyers to fight Germany. That would keep the Americans busy in the Pacific." My heart pounded as I awaited Hitler's response.

Hitler slowly nodded his head. "Yes, this makes sense to me. I will contact Hirohito. Hillman, your scientist should be a general in my army." Hitler removed the Eradicator from his pocket. No wonder I couldn't find it anywhere in the lab or in Hillman's home! Hitler held the device and ordered me to "Make more of them." With that, Hitler handed the Eradicator to Hillman, stood up, abruptly returned to his car, and was quickly driven off. Hillman and I had never seen eye-to-eye on anything, but for that one moment after Hitler's departure, I think we did. Hillman knew what I knew: Hitler was impossible to please, and most likely insane.

I was feeling pretty good. Hillman had persuaded Hitler to break the non-aggression pact with Russia, and I might have influenced Hitler to pressure Japan to enter the war sooner. Hillman and I had a "normal" discussion before we left Berchtesgarten. I casually asked, "Did you tell Hitler you were from the future?"

Hillman confidently exclaimed, "Of course I did. I gave him a detailed explanation of his thousand-year Reich reaching its two hundredth birthday." When Hillman told me this,

I remember saying to myself that Hitler would be more overconfident than ever. This also could work to the Allies' advantage.

I spent the next several months stalling the Eradicator program as best I could. I kept telling Hillman I couldn't make any more Eradicator weapons without more of the meteorite. Truth be told, I had no idea if this meteorite had the correct elements to construct any weapons at all. This was not my field of expertise. The lab equipment was too crude to find out anything definitive. So Hillman played cat and mouse with Hitler, while I played cat and mouse with him.

Strangely, there had been no word from North Africa, where Sigmund was sent with two of the SS goons. I was getting concerned and so was Hillman. Hillman would not let that Eradicator out of his sight. I asked if I could examine it more closely for one reason or another, but he never would let me even touch it. When Hillman left me alone in the lab, I spent my time constructing a copy of the chrome chip which made the Eradicator work. I wanted to be ready at a moment's notice, if the opportunity ever presented itself, to exchange the chips. If so, I could render the Eradicator useless.

CHAPTER 10
FAILURE AND SUCCESS

One day Gestapo agents brought a British spy to our lab. I had a horrible feeling in my stomach, as I suspected what was to come. Hillman arrived minutes later with Hitler. The Fuehrer wanted to see a demonstration of the Eradicator on a non-Jew. The look in the eye of that British agent is a memory I will take to my grave. This demonstration was horrible enough to have to watch, but Hillman made it even worse. He wanted to test my loyalty, which he (correctly) still questioned. Hillman nodded to the two Gestapo agents, who moved towards me and put Lugers to my head as Hillman handed me the Eradicator. He wanted me to kill the British agent in front of Hitler.

I was sick to my stomach. The idea briefly crossed my mind to try to kill Hitler with the Eradicator, but the stream that the Eradicator fires takes a few seconds. Bullets leave their chamber much faster; I couldn't have gotten a shot off in time. Logically, I knew that to protect my cover and help the Allied cause overall, I had to kill this innocent man standing five feet in front of me. I fired the weapon and then handed it back quickly to Hillman. All that remained were the poor man's clothes, some chemicals and bone fragments. Hitler watched with a large smile on his face. Hillman was always waiting for the compliment from Hitler, but it never came. Hitler turned to Hillman and said, "Do something about the bones, Hillman. I don't want to see any bones."

Perfect Hitler. What he should have viewed as the greatest weapon he had ever seen, he turned into a complaint. Hillman despondently said, "Yes, mein Fuehrer." Unfortunately, this was not the last test of the Eradicator that I would see. Weeks later Hillman and I were driven to a detention center. When we arrived, Hitler was there staring at his watch. Moments later ten men were marched out from the detention center to the roadside. Hitler wanted to see how many people the Eradicator could kill at one time. At least I didn't have to pull the trigger this time. Going from left to right, all the men were incinerated in seconds. Hitler commented again to Hillman about the bones not completely disappearing. But Hitler was pleased, and again returned to his Mercedes and was driven off.

This was a horrible day, but also a great day. On the car ride back to the lab, Hillman was lost in thought. I heard him mumble something about Hitler and the bones. I turned to Hillman at that moment of vulnerability and asked to see the Eradicator. "I think the guide stream is out of alignment," I told him.

Hillman handed me the weapon after he removed the firing pin. I took the chrome chip I had constructed in the lab from my pocket, quickly removed an outer ring from the chamber of the Eradicator, and made the switch. While working on the weapon, I also talked to Hillman about how hard it was to please Hitler. This distracted Hillman and kept him thinking about how desperately he wanted a compliment from Hitler.

Once I had rendered the Eradicator useless, I had to make my escape out of Germany. When Hillman discovered the Eradicator no longer worked, I would obviously be the chief suspect, and he would probably send the whole SS and Gestapo out to look for me.

I met Louise that evening to plan our escape. We argued for hours about where to go. Louise wanted to return to England, admittedly the more logical choice. I, on the other hand, wanted to find out what had happened to Sigmund Lloyd in North Africa. Louise finally gave in, though she knew in her heart and head that this was a mistake.

We used the computer to find where Rommel was most likely to be, and slowly made our way there. The trip seemed to take forever; it was a month or more before we arrived at Rommel's tent. The date was now late 1941. Louise and I had papers for both the SS and Gestapo. If we ran into SS officers we used our Gestapo papers, and vice versa. We also knew Hillman was sending agents all over Germany to look for me, but he did not know that I was traveling with a woman.

CHAPTER 11

THE DESERT FOX

We met Rommel just for one day, but what a strange day that was. Rommel was busy with his officers planning the attack on Egypt and attempted capture of the Suez Canal. I believe Rommel hated Hitler's war on innocents and unarmed objectors as much as I did.

At first, Louise and I had a problem getting an honest answer from Rommel and his officers. Rommel and his men believed we were Gestapo agents, because of our identity cards. The German military truly feared the Gestapo; most of Rommel's men wouldn't even make eye contact with me.

We had not asked any questions about Sigmund, as day turned to dusk. Rommel walked past me, commenting that we didn't act like Gestapo agents. When I asked him what he meant, Rommel looked up at me and said simply, "You haven't asked us any obnoxious questions yet."

I figured this was the perfect time to ask about Sigmund. "Field Marshal, I would like to ask you one question. Have you had contact with Sigmund Lloyd? He had long hair . . ."

Rommel cut off my conversation. "Yes, I knew who he was." My heart dropped into my stomach when Rommel said the word "was." Rommel must have seen my reaction, because he quickly asked me if Sigmund was a friend of mine. I nodded my head.

Rommel suddenly liked us, possibly because he liked Sigmund too. Rommel invited us to dinner in his tent. Just as we sat down to eat, in walked two real SS agents, who invited themselves to dinner.

Rommel and his top officer were not happy to see these two SS men, yet did not order them out of the tent. Apparently, they were going to have dinner with us after all. Louise and I were sure they were sent by Hillman to find me. Rommel tipped us off as to what had happened to Sigmund by saying to the SS agents, "Don't you think killing their friend, the long-haired historian, was a mistake?" Rommel wanted to see the SS and Gestapo get into some sort of confrontation right there in front of him. We were in a very awkward situation.

The SS agent seated across from me asked why I was wearing an Army captain's uniform if I was a member of the Gestapo. I said we used many different disguises to get information. That seemed enough of an explanation for the moment. Suddenly emboldened, I asked Rommel a question for all to hear. "Field Marshal, what exactly happened to Sigmund Lloyd?"

Rommel, after finishing a piece of bread he had been chewing on, replied, "He was shot dead by the SS man sitting across from you for questioning Adolph Hitler's sanity."

I was so angry, I began to reach for the Luger at my right side. Louise grabbed my arm under the table, to prevent me from doing something stupid. She truly was my protector. She had orders from Churchill not to let anything happen to me. The SS agent who shot Sigmund then spoke up, "The Fuehrer is our god, and to question his vision is punishable by death. I simply carried out his sentence."

Louise, probably to stop me from doing something I'd regret, stood up at this moment and asked to see the two SS agents privately, outside of Rommel's tent. I had no idea what she was planning. Both SS men complied with her request, and followed her out of the tent. Rommel raised an eyebrow at me, and continued to eat his dinner. Suddenly, without a word being heard from outside the tent, two shots were fired. Louise calmly returned to the tent, sat down, put her napkin back on her lap and said, "I carried out their sentence for killing Professor Lloyd."

Rommel smiled, and then noticed that his second-in-command had stood and drawn his gun, obviously to arrest Louise. Rommel gestured for him to sit back down. Rommel calmly said, "It's a shame those two had to kill each other. I wonder what it was about."

Rommel will always have my gratitude for the way he handled that situation. We spoke briefly, and under mutual agreement, Louise and I left North Africa shortly thereafter. We then traveled north via German troop transport trains. It was interesting to hear the soldiers' worries about the new front with Russia. We also read that a United States destroyer called the *Greer* had been attacked off of Iceland by a German U-boat. President Roosevelt made a declaration regarding any American shipping that would be attacked: Germany would do so at its own peril.

On the quieter moments of the train ride, my thoughts were with Sigmund Lloyd and what a useless death he had suffered. I never learned the exact sequence of events that led to his being shot by the SS agent, yet wondered how Sigmund could have called Hitler insane in front of one of those fanatics. He was much smarter than that. It just made no sense to me. In any event, I had lost my closest friend. I also briefly wondered about the stupid meteorite that sent Sigmund to North Africa in the first place. Rommel made no mention of it, and Louise and I forgot to ask about it. Who knows? Perhaps there was no larger piece of the meteorite to analyze anyway. One thing was certain: there was no threat Hillman would create any Eradicator weapons.

We traveled into Holland and headed for the coast, where Louise had many contacts in the Underground. It was relatively easy for us to cross the channel in a fishing boat. Now my thoughts turned to Kartov. He was so isolated and alone in Russia. We had no way to contact him, and he probably didn't know where we were, either. After losing Sigmund, I prayed Kartov would have a better fate. I hoped Mac could find a way to get word to Kartov somehow.

CHAPTER 12
CHURCHILL'S DILEMMA

When we made our way back to London command head-quarters, there was a lot going on. It was late November 1941, and Mac had deciphered some internal Japanese code. Mac and I embraced; it had been almost a year since we had seen each other. I then told him of Sigmund's fate. Mac got weak in the knees and had to sit down. So much was happening all at once. Mac didn't have time to grieve, as he was heading to meet Churchill to discuss the newly broken Japanese code. Mac invited me to join them, which I did. On our way over, Mac explained the delicate nature of his discovery.

Even Churchill wasn't certain how best to proceed. Mac had decoded the date for the Japanese attack on Pearl Harbor, and relayed it to Churchill. The problem was whether to tell President Roosevelt. It was thought if the Americans knew the date of the attack they might delay or prevent it, and if they did, America might not join the war in Europe as quickly. Churchill grappled with this for days, then decided on a compromise plan. He told Roosevelt to get all four of his aircraft carriers out of Pearl Harbor between the weeks of December 1 and December 14.

Now we waited to see how and when the Americans would join the global war effort. Mac had also told Churchill of a new weapon that could destroy an entire city with one bomb. Mac and I were clearly doing all we could think of. Louise was extremely curious about my relationship with Mac. She sensed that neither of us seemed to fit in, but she couldn't put her finger on why. Louise used to tell me Mac and I either knew too much or too little in certain situations. It did seem to drive her crazy, but at this point, we weren't ready for full disclosure with her.

This was an easy time for me. I worked with Mac breaking the German codes for ground and air operations on the Eastern front. We had to look busy but these codes were in our handheld units, so honestly, there was no work to be done. The problem was that even though we had broken these codes, there weren't enough weapons and men to do anything with this knowledge. So in many cases, despite knowing all of the German troop movements and deployments in advance, the Russians lost most of these battles due to lack of men or materiel.

We decoded a radio message from the Japanese ambassador to Berlin, reporting that if Japan were attacked by the United States, Germany would declare war immediately on the United States. When Mac told this to Churchill, he just smiled. Louise was given another assignment back in Germany, and I wasn't happy about it. I was getting possessive toward Louise, which made no sense, but one can't question one's feelings. We embraced before she left. I promised to tell her the entire truth one day. I wasn't to see her again for many years.

Mac and I talked strategy around that time. We felt we had done as much as we could in Europe. What we needed to do next was help the Americans develop the atomic bomb before Germany did. We then got word that, by the narrowest of margins, the American Congress had amended their neutrality act. Now merchant ships were allowed to be armed and given passage into war zones. This was good news to be sure, but in Europe it was felt that America was moving at a snail's pace.

When Japan attacked Pearl Harbor on December 7, 1941, the global war really began to take shape. Churchill expected America to declare war on Japan and Germany at the same time, but this did not happen. Days passed and no declaration of war on Germany was forthcoming. It appeared Hitler had to make the first move and thankfully, for every non-fascist on Earth, he did just that. On December 11, Hitler declared war on the United States. This was no doubt the greatest blunder of the war. Hitler could have waited a year or more before declaring war on America, as he had done in our timeline.

CHAPTER 13

HITLER'S BLUNDER

Hitler kept his word to the Japanese ambassador, and I felt that maybe I had had something to do with it, when I lunched with Hitler in Berchtesgarten. Churchill knew America would make countless mistakes in the first months of the war. "They aren't battle-ready yet, but they have the greatest war machine potential on Earth. We will surely win."

Hitler had given Roosevelt what he needed to get involved in Europe and finally push the pacifists in America aside. Once the United States became committed to this war, eleven months earlier than it had happened in our timeline, we knew our final job here in the past was to assist the Americans in atomic research. Mac got permission from Churchill to leave for America and work on the atomic bomb research project. I traveled with Mac to America. We made sure to travel across the Atlantic Ocean on a ship that the German U-Boats did not sink. Handy little devices, were those historical computers. Before we left England, Churchill told Mac that in ten days he was coming to Washington to begin talks with Roosevelt about a coordinated war effort plan.

Mac told me Kartov had a severely injured leg and would try to get word to us, somehow, in America. Mac also told me Kartov was the planner of the slash-and-burn policy the Russian people deployed as the German army approached Moscow. I thought that Clem Rizzoli might be able to help us contact Kartov once we reached America. I was very much looking forward to seeing Clem again. I missed that short, stocky, foul-mouthed Brooklynite.

CHAPTER 14

MAC'S LOVE OF AMERICA

As I had hoped, Clem Rizzoli met us at the dock in New York. After he and Mac introduced themselves, we moved to Clem's limousine and headed back to Washington. On the ride down to the American capital, Mac told Clem he had further work to do in the code-breaking department. Clem, with his amazing use of the English language, said to Mac, "Help us build this fucking bomb first." Mac gave me a look and I just laughed. What would take other men paragraphs to say, Mr. Rizzoli could impart in just a few words.

Mac was amazed on the ride to Washington by how little this war had touched the American people. Mac thought he was in Shangri-La, that mythical place of peace untouched by war or crime. America was so fortunate that they had not been attacked on their mainland, so the country could go to full-time war production without fear of bombing runs by their enemies. Once we reached Washington, we were debriefed. We informed the military leaders present that we had neutralized the second Eradicator so it was now useless. This made everyone in the room very happy. Clem asked me quite directly, "So are you fucking telling me that the Nazis can't build anymore of these fucking things?"

I said, "Yes, that is correct."

Clem was so happy with this news, he invited Mac and me back to his home in northern Virginia for dinner. That was the most fun I had ever had in my life, having dinner at Clem

Rizzoli's house. He had five children, all less than 10 years old. Clem's wife was very attractive, but she had a fouler mouth than Clem did, which I thought impossible. The house was a complete mess when we arrived.

Mac and I thought we understood the English language, until we entered the world of Clem Rizzoli and his wife, Kathy. Mac had his mouth open for most of the evening, as the expletives were being thrown around by Clem and his wife. I don't remember all of it, but I never laughed so hard in my life. It started when Kathy screamed at Clem when we came through the front door of the house.

"Guests!? You brought fucking guests without telling me?! What are you, fucking retarded? The house is a mess, I got no food for these guys, and you are a total asshole." You get the picture. The whole evening was like that. I never had more fun just sitting and watching something in my life.

Clem apologized to us as he drove us to a local hotel for the evening. Mac dryly commented he was surprised that Clem and Kathy hadn't killed each other by now. Clem got defensive. "Hey, I love that broad. I'd do anything for her. Sure, we scream at each other, but that don't mean nothing." As Clem dropped us off, he informed me that we would be working under a brigadier general named Leslie Groves, who had just been put in charge of this secret operation called the Manhattan Project.

Mac and I were not nuclear scientists, but we did have a list of all the materials needed to complete an atomic bomb. We also had the equations in our handheld computers. The Americans would have to build the centrifuges and tubes, then complete the conversion process for turning uranium-238 into uranium-235 and then into plutonium-239. We were sent to Los Alamos, New Mexico with ten other scientists from around the globe to work on this project. Mac and I did not do much other than help give the scientists the right formula, and correct a formula that was off by a molecule or two. Mac had a lot of experience from his days in the London cipher division in finding ways for others to take the credit for discoveries. He taught me that talent as well.

I remember working with a man named Eugene Wigner, a Hungarian physicist, as well as a Chinese-American woman named W.V. Chien-Shiung. They were both highly intelligent people who were clearly on the right track. The story of our first meeting with Teller and Einstein was priceless. Robert Oppenheimer was the head of the project; he reported to the brigadier general.

Let me backtrack a day or so. Clem took us to the airport for our flight to New Mexico. Clem said in the car, "Wait until you meet Einstein. He talks with that German accent like you guys." Mac and I both knew of Einstein's accomplishments from history, which were not easy to find out. His contributions to science were eliminated from our history books, when he came to America when Hitler took power in 1933, and was considered a deserter by the Nazi high command. It was only because of Sigmund's extensive research of the period that we were able to know the truth. Mac and I both looked forward to meeting him. Clem hit us with an unexpected statement as we were getting out of the car at the airport. He asked us, "You know that Eradicator had components that are not in our periodic table. Care to share?"

I decided to say straight out, "The weapon was made from a meteorite that crash-landed in 2078." With that, I closed the car door and left Clem with a surprised look on his face.

There was a mix-up at the airport in Albuquerque. Our plane had been delayed twice, and whoever was supposed to meet us missed us somehow. Anyway, Mac and I took a cab to Los Alamos. Before we went to the base, Mac wanted to go shopping so we would better blend in with the inhabitants in this city. I did not feel this necessary, but Mac insisted.

CHAPTER 15
MEETING ALBERT EINSTEIN

We went to a clothing store where we each bought dungaree jeans, button-down Western shirts, and cowboy boots. I felt I looked ridiculous, but Mac thought we looked great. He loved America, he just loved it here. The freedom of transport and the lack of fear on people's faces made Mac so happy. He actually made me happier just being with him and his incredibly upbeat persona. After picking up a pizza to go, a cab dropped us off at the gate of this "secret facility" that all the local people seemed to know about. A guard checked our papers, then opened the gate and allowed us entry. Mac did have to explain, though, why he was carrying a pizza box. Finally the guard said, "Second building on the left."

Mac knocked on the door and Albert Einstein answered it. Mac's face dropped in awe at meeting one of the greatest scientists in history. Mac looked at Einstein and said, "You're Albert Einstein!"

Einstein did not answer Mac, but handed him a five dollar bill. "What's this for?" Mac asked.

Einstein said, "The pizza." That was our introduction to Albert Einstein. Mac and I had plenty of free time and not much to actually do. We waited for one of the other ten scientists to stumble on the right idea, and then we'd advance that idea so they would get closer to the correct equations.

Mac was getting used to operating in this way, because it was more or less exactly what he had been doing in London with the German Enigma codes. He gave credit to others for breaking the codes as he pointed the various decoders in the right direction. I wanted to do more, but Mac kept talking me out of it. The scientists were clearly making progress, and I estimated that we were only weeks away from having all the formulas corrected. Then we could begin to build the actual components necessary to produce an atomic bomb. The urgency was that Hillman now had Sigmund's computer with him, so the Nazis now had access to the same information about building the A-bomb as we did.

The most interesting part of our time in New Mexico were the evening conversations after dinner. Usually, four or five scientists would gather to talk politics, the ethics of building this horrific weapon, or even baseball. This is where Mac began to get interested in America's pastime. I was much more interested in the ethics conversations regarding what we were attempting to do in New Mexico. Mac and I usually took the lead in trying to convince these scientists that we had to beat Hitler to this weapon or the free world would cease to exist. Teller was very concerned that the world was opening a door that could never be closed again. He was right, of course, but clearly there was no choice. We knew from first-hand experience that America had to build this bomb.

One evening after dinner, Einstein came to our cabin and sat down in the comfortable chair. Each cabin had one comfortable chair; the others were bridge chairs. Anyway, Mac and I were unprepared for the after-dinner topic Einstein brought up.

Einstein was an extremely curious man. Without asking, he would look in your drawers or peek in your attaché case, that sort of thing. Apparently, while on one of his scavenger hunts, Einstein found Mac's handheld computer. While seated in the "good chair" Einstein said to us, while I was cleaning our dinner dishes, "I came across your miniature informational historical encyclopedia. What I did was a terrible intrusion of your privacy. And I would like to apologize."

Mac and I just looked at each other. We had no idea how much information Einstein had accessed. I think I mumbled something like, "Oh, that's all right."

Then Einstein said, "There are two possible conclusions one could draw from what I read in your device. One is that you are science-fiction writers with incredible imaginations; the other is that you are both from the future. How am I doing so far?"

Einstein noticed that we were at a loss for words, which made him think his assertions may have been true. So he continued, "I have come to several conclusions about the two of you. Would you like to hear my theory?"

Mac got excited to hear Einstein's analysis of the situation. Mac grabbed a chair and sat down opposite Einstein. "Shoot," Mac exclaimed.

"I have determined that the components in your devices are at least 50 years ahead of present-day technology. I also examined the Eradicator weapon of which you are both acquainted. It contains elements not as yet found on Earth. How am I doing so far?"

Mac had much looser lips than I did. He insisted on telling Einstein the whole truth, under the stipulation that Einstein could tell no one else without our permission. Mac casually stated, "Churchill knows, so why not Einstein?"

Albert Einstein sat there completely mesmerized by what we told him over the course of the next few hours. Einstein said "unbelievable" many times as he listened to our story. When we finally brought Einstein up-to-date he remarked, "Do you think you have done enough to change the war's outcome?"

Mac gave Einstein a real pep talk as he said, "That is where you come in, Professor. With your help we build this bomb first, then deploy it, end this war, and stop the Nazis forever." Einstein seemed renewed when he left our cabin that evening. I don't think he was 100 percent behind the building of the weapon until that night. Now he was the first to show up in the morning and the last to leave at night. Since we had now shared our full knowledge with Einstein, we were able to move much faster in construction of the special alloyed tubes and centrifuges. Einstein no longer questioned every small detail to make sure it was thoroughly tested, as he had been doing up until this point. He knew the equations we had provided were correct, so it was full steam ahead.

We came to trust Einstein so much that we let him read from our handheld computer from time to time. He enjoyed reading about how history changed, and what sequences and events were to follow. Einstein was not happy to read about his own death, however. This quite understandably upset him. The Americans in our timeline had to surrender Einstein to the Nazis or lose another city to nuclear attack. Einstein was dangerous to the Nazis because of his knowledge of nuclear physics. President Truman reluctantly complied, and Einstein was shot by the Gestapo in northern Mexico in 1946. At this point, Einstein put the handheld computer down and mumbled, "I think I've read enough for a while."

Clem Rizzoli came out to see how we were getting along with all the other "egg heads," as he so eloquently called us. I told him that we had done as much as our limited knowledge of nuclear fission had allowed us to. I assured Clem that the consortium of scientists was well on its way to a successful test of the atomic bomb. Clem seemed to know all about it, as he told us a special B-29 bomber was being built to carry this atomic weapon. Clem then told us that there was to be a secret meeting in Teheran between the big three, FDR, Churchill, and Stalin, at the end of November 1943. Mac and I got very excited. We wanted to go. This was the first time since the Bolshevik revolution in 1917 that Stalin was leaving Russian soil.

Clem knew we would want to go after he told us Kartov would be coming as one of Stalin's advisors. We hadn't seen Victor Kartov in over five years, since we had split up in that basement in Berlin in 1938. We said our goodbyes to Einstein, and off we went to Teheran.

CHAPTER 16
SEEING VICTOR AGAIN

It took forever to reach Teheran; we took a strange route to get there for security reasons. When we saw Victor for the first time, Mac and I were shocked by his appearance. Kartov walked with a one arm crutch, he had a scraggily beard, and looked gaunt. I think he had lost forty pounds since we had last seen him. My first thought was that Mac and I had much easier assignments than poor Victor.

When we first made eye contact, we teared up during our long hug. We spoke for hours about what we all had been through over the past five years. Victor was one of five men who had Stalin's ear; he clearly had done his job in our attempt to revise history. Churchill told Mac at the conference that fifteen British scientists were being sent to America to assist in the A-bomb effort. When we mentioned this to Kartov, he did not act surprised. Kartov, at first hesitantly, told us one of those fifteen scientists was in fact a Russian spy. Stalin was concerned that after the war, the West might have a nuclear weapon and Russia would not.

Mac and I weren't sure what to do, if anything. We assumed that Russia and the United States and Britain were all allies, so if everyone shared the technology that would be all right. I suppose this might have been the moment that your cold war between the Soviet Union and the West actually began. Mac and I were extremely naive regarding East/West politics at that time. In any event, Mac and I said nothing and this Russian agent joined the A-bomb project in New Mexico.

We had a good time during this conference. The Americans and British worked out an agreement to bomb Germany day and night. Churchill made promises of American weapons to help in the fighting in Russia, which the American generals objected to. When the meetings were over, Churchill asked Mac to come back to England and continue his cryptology work. Mac asked me if it was okay that we split up again. I told him to go. Clem Rizzoli was standing next to me when Mac asked me this, so I suppose Clem felt obligated to ask me to come back to the United States because I was needed there.

I did agree to return with Clem, although I had no idea what else I could possibly do to help the war effort. I soon realized that Clem just wanted me close to him, as he had many questions and few answers. I had a very sad and uneasy feeling when I said goodbye to Victor. I sensed deep down that I would never see him again. It was just a feeling, but one that I couldn't shake. Victor was so frail looking, with his broken knee-cap and one armed crutch. Victor's parting words to me were, "I'll see you on the other side." I wasn't sure if Victor meant the other side after the war ended, or the other side of the Atlantic Ocean, or the other side of life itself.

I don't want to get out of chronological sequence in telling my life story, but Victor and I had no idea how prophetic those words were. I had no such negative feeling regarding Mac's return to England. A few months later Mac got word to me that the heavy water plant that the Germans were constructing in Norway had been destroyed by a daring partisan attack. I knew that Germany had lost the race to complete the atomic bomb, and thus the Nazi defeat in the war was sure to follow.

CHAPTER 17

FRIENDSHIP

Mac had broken all the German codes; this not only worked for decoding their internal messages, but also enabled Mac to feed the Germans false information. As D-day approached in early June 1944, Mac kept sending messages that the Americans were landing in Calais. The Germans reinforced Calais, pulling troops from Normandy and other possible landing sites. Mac had truly done an extraordinary job for the Allied cause.

I, on the other hand, was invited back to the United States, and honestly had very little on my plate. My involvement with anything related to this war was clearly over. Clem Rizzoli had graciously invited me to stay at his house, since I had no place to stay in Washington. I stayed with Clem and his wife and five screaming children for two weeks or so before other opportunities presented themselves. Clem's family life was so chaotic, I couldn't think in that house. I had never experienced anything like it in my lifetime. Even something as simple as "pass the salt" turned into an argument. I had to laugh. The cursing was non-stop but seemed to be their family's method of communication, nothing more sinister than that. Even the kids used four-letter words.

One night after dinner, Clem asked me to take a walk with him. As we walked through his neighborhood he asked me, "So you're a time traveler, huh?"

Clem clearly caught me off guard. "Where'd you hear that?"

Clem simply responded that he had his sources. I supposed Churchill might have told President Roosevelt, who told Clem. However Clem had found this out, I didn't think he was fishing for information he did not already have, so I decided to tell him everything.

Clem listened intently; he asked intelligent questions and did not act shocked or surprised by what he was hearing, as Einstein had. Clem was level-headed under all circumstances, except perhaps in his own household. It was easy to think of Clem Rizzoli as a lesser mind if you based intelligence on vocabulary alone, but Clem was highly intelligent. I would never underestimate him.

Clem asked what I intended to do after the war was over. I honestly hadn't given it much thought. Our sole mission was to change the outcome of the war. Since I had no answer for Clem, I decided to ask him the same question. Clem smiled, "I've got some offers for some deep cover stuff. Who knows, I may knock on your door one day."

Our friendship had reached the point of full disclosure, so I asked him, "What will become of the Eradicator? I hope your government doesn't try to mass-produce them. This was the chosen weapon of my reality's Gestapo. They would simply make their enemies disappear."

"You know we can't duplicate that chip in it. Don't sweat it, Doc. It's locked away tight." Clem smiled and asked me how I liked staying in his house the last few weeks.

"Entertaining," was my answer. Clem smiled and told me that he had a surprise for me. First he handed me the keys to a room in a swanky Washington D.C. four-star hotel.

When I tried to ask what he was handing me, he then gave me his car keys and told me, "Shut the fuck up and just go."

I complied with Clem's eloquent request. When I got to the hotel, I assumed Clem was just giving me some time away from his family, but it was more. Much more.

I heard the shower running when I entered the room. A suitcase was positioned in the corner and a robe was on the bed. My first thought was that Clem had hired a prostitute for me. Then I thought to myself, why would a prostitute need a suitcase full of clothes? I didn't know whether to leave the room or not, when suddenly out walked a naked Louise from the shower. She was momentarily stunned, as she thought she was alone, and then she just smiled and put her robe on, and returned to the bathroom. Clem had gotten Louise assigned to a liaison position in Washington so we could be together. I was so happy and thankful. To go from the insanity of Clem's house to total bliss was as good as it gets. I must confess, I felt a bit guilty. Mac was still working in London as the war was winding down, and poor Kartov, whom we had not heard from in some time, had been having such a tough time of it. I got over my guilt in short order.

Clem got us a government rental house to live in. Once again, I wasn't certain if Louise really liked me or if she was doing this because she was ordered to. This time around with Louise, I woke up and "smelled the coffee" as you Americans like to say. It occurred to me that I didn't care. This was too good to screw up by being jealous or possessive. Louise and I spent the final months of the war together in that rental house. We went sightseeing, shopping, and talking. I soon realized, however, that my handheld unit was running out of paper, as I had been printing various currencies for years. I decided to ask Clem for a big favor. I needed him to get me several small rolls of U.S. government paper, the kind you make all of your dollars from. The paper I had used previously from my timeline had a setting for any currencies' thickness or denomination, though clearly most of my world used Deutschmarks.

Clem laughed when I asked him this favor. He said, "You know I've put guys in prison for trying to do what you're doing. Well, I guess I'll have to arrest myself." Clem was able to get me paper with the necessary threads per inch to create U.S. dollars, but he also converted 100 small rolls that fit my unit perfectly. When Clem handed me the large suitcase with all the rolls in it, he simply said, "You deserve this for keeping my kids from speaking freaking German."

A few days later Clem called to tell me President Roosevelt was very sick. Two days later, Roosevelt was dead. The Germans and Japanese tried to turn his death into a propaganda victory for the Axis powers, but clearly Germany and Japan were in full retreat at this point in the war. Mac later told me that Churchill was concerned the new president, Harry Truman, might try to negotiate a peace immediately after Roosevelt's death, and not finish the job. Those concerns proved false indeed, once Churchill had spoken with Truman by telephone. Churchill told Mac he had no doubt that "that little fireplug of a man would finish this war, and soon."

Rumors were flying everywhere that Truman would use the atomic bomb, which was now tested and ready to deploy, on Germany. The Allies felt Germany was virtually defeated already, without this weapon. Many felt that rumor was enough to force Germany to surrender, which they did in short order. Japan was another matter. Clem came by my house after Germany surrendered and discussed what he knew of the impending use of the A-bomb on Japan. Clem told me the American high command had turned down a proposal to detonate the bomb on a deserted island, a plan which Clem had favored. Giving advance warning to Japanese leaders was also decided against, for fear that American prisoners of war would be moved to that location before the detonation.

Churchill gave Truman a pep talk and the confidence to use the weapon against Japan. Churchill told Truman that Japan had sneak-attacked America to start this war and the Americans had every right to finish it. Finish it the Americans did. When those bombs fell on Hiroshima and Nagasaki, I fell back into my chair and said to myself that we had done it. All future history would now have to start anew.

CHAPTER 18

MISSION ACCOMPLISHED: NOW WHAT?

I watched the jubilant celebrations in New York City, as the war was now over. I can't describe fully what I felt standing on the sidewalks of New York, but the smile stayed on my face for weeks. Mac came to America a month later. Louise said that she had to return to London, to tie up all of her "loose ends." I asked her when she would return. Louise somberly said, "I don't know." I wasn't sure if I'd ever see Louise again, so as a last plea I offered to marry her. Louise smiled, rubbed my face gently and said, "We'll see." She left, and a day later Mac arrived. I liked Mac a lot, but to use your national pastime's expression, this was a terrible trade of Louise for Mac in my life.

Suddenly, Mac and I had no historical advanced knowledge. A new timeline was taking shape. Our handheld units were now only good for printing money or copies of identification cards. Mac stayed in the Washington house with me for a few weeks. You never really know a person until you live with them. Boy, was he a slob. I knew that we could not live together long-term. Mac wanted to write a book about what we had just accomplished. I talked him out of that idea. We needed to let this new world order evolve on its own, without such a shocking tale to threaten its beginnings.

I wanted to work in science in some way. Mac, on the other hand, decided to never work again. He felt we had saved the world from a horrible future and deserved to relax. He had a point. Thanks to Clem getting me all those extra rolls of government paper, we'd have enough money for a lifetime. Mac moved to Boston. He had fallen in love with the game of baseball, and the Boston Red Sox in particular. Every time we spoke, the name "Ted Williams" came up.

Mac's goal in the year 1946 was to go to every major league baseball stadium to see a game. I thought this was an incredible waste of time, but also realized Mac was so happy doing this that I had no right to rain on his parade. Mac and I had not heard from Kartov, and were getting concerned. I asked Clem to look into the matter. Clem called me a day later to say he was sorry to tell us that Victor Kartov had been killed during a German bombing run in the last weeks of the war. The Russians weren't very forthcoming with their causality lists of high officials. Clem had to use private channels to get this information.

What a shame. We had lost Sigmund and now Kartov, both in somewhat meaningless deaths. Mac and I then spoke of Hillman and the Eradicator. We both felt that the Eradicator was in safe hands, at least for now. As for Hillman, Mac and I were divided on what to do about him. Clem thought he had escaped to Brazil, but that was only a rumor. In any event, Mac and I didn't do anything about Hillman, though we were concerned he might find us one day.

I postponed my job hunt until after 1946, to keep Mac company as he traveled from stadium to stadium. I've lived many interesting years in my life, but I cannot think of a more meaningless one, though Mac and I did have fun. That was the year I became a regular user of antacids, after eating in various baseball parks. Mac loved Americans, and he loved baseball. I was a bit shocked when he started yelling at players during games; I suppose his assimilation was complete. After the 1946 baseball season ended, I took an apartment in New York City. I then started toying around with a new and improved telescope design, working out of my apartment.

CHAPTER 19

MY SHORT-LIVED
TELESCOPE BUSINESS

Mac went back to his small house in Boston. What, if anything, he was doing at that time I had no idea. I finished a new prototype design for a high-powered telescope using some of what I had learned from my early training in advanced optics. There was an energetic young man named Todd in my building who stopped in to see me one day. He took notice of the telescope, and asked me a thousand questions. Then he got all excited and said something about us being partners. Then he left. I honestly didn't give him much thought until he rang my bell ten days later with orders for one hundred of my telescopes. He was hitting every specialty store in New York.

I had no intention of full-time employment, but suddenly I had to open a small factory in Queens to mass-produce these telescopes. I was now a businessman. The young man was my junior partner, and he deserved it. What a hustler he was. I remember in early 1947 when he flew to Los Angeles and got orders for ten thousand telescopes. I was shocked by that order. Ten thousand people were that interested in stargazing? I felt this was truly amazing. I was very proud of the fact that I was making real money and providing a service to the American people. As an added bonus I was able to put my counterfeiting machine away for awhile, making me feel better, because I was supporting myself financially.

81

I decided to fly out to Los Angeles to see for myself where all these telescopes were going. I went to my junior partner's new penthouse apartment in Beverly Hills. What a beautiful apartment it was, with windows on three sides, and several telescopes on tripods situated in front of the open windows. Todd was truly thrilled and excited to see me. At least at first. As the late afternoon turned into the early evening, things became much clearer to me.

To my shock and dismay, it appeared that Todd had been pitching my telescopes to people as a way to spy on their neighbors. Twenty-five people came over that evening, taking turns looking at half-naked people walking around their homes. I decided to make a business arrangement with Todd in the coming months, for him to buy me out of the business. I honestly didn't want my name associated with this use of my advanced adaptation. I sold Todd all of my patents and the factory kept running as before, with Todd in full control. I just walked away with my head held high. Mac, of course, thought I was a total prude and nuts to leave this lucrative vocation, but as my uncle used to say, "A man's gotta do what lets him sleep at night."

CHAPTER 20

ALIENS ON EARTH

It was now early July 1947, and I had just returned home from a few hours relaxing at Jones Beach when my doorbell rang. What a great and pleasant surprise it was to see Clem's face at my door! I had no idea that my life was about to take a turn no one could have foreseen. Clem told me that a spaceship had crashed in New Mexico, and he wanted my input. I thought he was kidding at first, but Clem didn't curse once, so I knew he was dead serious. I quickly asked if Mac could come too. Clem said, "Not on this trip. I had enough trouble getting one civilian approved."

On our flight to New Mexico I sensed a tenseness from Clem that I had never seen before. He was in charge of this mess, as he put it, and was asked to do a cover-up, which just didn't sit right with him. When we got to the site, we met with a man named Jesse Marcel. The three of us went over to the crash site. Most of the debris and bodies had already been taken to the 8th Air Force Base in Texas. We took the short flight to Fort Worth. Clem asked me if I had seen any alien life forms or heard of them in the future. I said "no," which was the truth.

Apparently it was a violent thunderstorm that had brought the aliens' silver saucer-shaped disc down. I was anxious to see the spacecraft and the alien bodies when we got to the airbase. As his cover story, Clem said that a weather balloon had crash-landed, leaving shreds of aluminum foil everywhere.

Many of the local farmers in the area had seen more than they should have, as Clem put it. Clem was correct when he said, "This story can't be covered up completely, and rumors will be flying for years." On the flight to Fort Worth, Clem apologized to me for bringing me into this investigation. I supposed there were no other scientists he knew personally and trusted with top security clearance. I simply told Clem that I was glad to help, since I had nothing to do anyway.

When we arrived at the airbase, there was already an autopsy underway on one of the four alien bodies that had been recovered. The elliptical eyes frightened me, at least initially. The bodies were no more than four feet tall, completely hairless, with a grey tint to them. Clem wanted me to examine the saucer itself. The microchip technology was far more advanced than anything I'd seen, even in my time, and certainly 500 years ahead of present-day Earth technology.

For the next six months, my job was analyzing everything found on that alien vessel. I knew microchip technology would take several decades to reverse-engineer and implement into society, but I was able to begin the process that others would complete. Clem was involved in some top-secret base being created to deal with "alien issues" as Clem put it. I had no idea that in the years to come I would get to meet live aliens from various different planets.

CHAPTER 21
MAC'S GIFT

Clem had finally given me permission to discuss what I was doing with Mac, but *only* Mac. Clem was in charge of security regarding all things related to alien visitation on Earth. I decided I wanted to tell Mac in person about this, so I was given permission to fly to Boston to see him. The time was October of 1948. Mac told me he was going to the Boston Red Sox versus the Cleveland Indians one-game playoff for the American League pennant. I was to meet him that evening after the game. This was when I was going to discuss the work I had been doing for the past many months.

Mac called me at his house, as I was waiting for him there. He vehemently complained about the Red Sox losing to Cleveland, and angrily mumbled something about the owner of the Cleveland Indians giving out free nylons to the female patrons at the game, to sway influence in the Indians' favor. He also spoke negatively of a Cleveland Indians player name Lou Boudreau, who hit two home runs. I told him to drive safely; he was clearly out of his head with overzealous fan anger.

The drive from Fenway Park to Mac's home should have taken less than half an hour. Three hours later, he still hadn't come home. I called the local police department. The police told me that there were accidents all over town, no doubt from frustrated Red Sox fans. I gave them Mac's license plate number and asked them to call me if they heard anything. An hour later the police did call me. Mac had had an accident with a cement truck and was in critical condition. What a nightmare that was. When I got to the hospital, Mac was in a coma. His prognosis was dismal at best.

I sat for days at Mac's bedside. I told Clem what had happened, so he gave me whatever time I needed. I thought that with the possible exception of Hillman, I was the only one left from the future. I felt so alone. A moment of levity happened one day when Mac's doctor came in and asked if I knew any reason why Mac may have been driving erratically before his accident. "Yeah," I said, "the Red Sox lost that playoff game."

The doctor laughed and said, "Yeah, we had a few fans in intensive care that night."

Then I made a joke that turned out to be the truth. I told the doctor that, knowing Mac, he'd come out of his coma on the opening day of the baseball season in 1949. Sure enough, the first Monday in April 1949, Mac came out of his coma. What I had not expected was Mac's new "gift" that accompanied his return to consciousness. When he came out of his coma, the doctor called me and I came immediately to the hospital. I had been flying back and forth between the secret base in Nevada and Boston over the past year. Fortunately, I was in Boston when Mac awoke. I went through most of the money I had gotten from selling the telescope business to pay Mac's doctor bills.

When I got to Mac's room, he was groggy but excited to see me. He seemed like the old Mac to me, at first, with no sign of brain damage. Mac then gestured for me to come closer, and he whispered, "I know what happens to people when they die." I thought he was half dreaming, so I didn't think much of what he said at first. A few days later, the doctor said I could take Mac home, but to keep an eye on him. Mac regained his strength quickly, and that's when my life permanently entered the "Twilight Zone." Mac went on and on about the souls of the dead being thankful to the two of us for changing history. Now I was sure he had suffered brain damage from a lack of oxygen. My goal, early on, was to humor him and hope that he came back to himself.

CHAPTER 22

THE RELL, THE DELP, AND THE ZERA

However, Mac was relentless and persistent in what he said. He gave me intricate stories with incredible detail. I found myself beginning to believe him. Then I thought if I took him to a baseball game that might snap him out of it. I took him to an early season Red Sox game against the Yankees. Mac hardly watched any of the game; he talked my ear off for three hours about things so strange to a scientist's mind, I got a headache trying to understand him. Here are some of the key points he tried to make:

The souls of the dead were protecting the living from alien races that exist on a two-dimensional plane. These aliens have not yet figured out a way to penetrate the dimension of the dead, so they could not take control of the living, and thus take some form of control over planet Earth. Mac also told me that he was in constant contact with the souls of the dead. I selfishly did like when he kept telling me that the souls of the dead were very thankful to us for altering Earth's history, thus saving billions of souls from horrible deaths. Mac said there was much more to the puzzle, and that he had just touched the surface.

I figured this was as good a time as any to tell Mac what I had been doing. Mac was not only fascinated by the alien remains and spacecraft that I had been working on, but also convinced that my work tied in with his new gift somehow. Clem gave me permission to bring Mac out to a new base in Groom Lake, Nevada, later called Area 51, where things got even more bizarre, if such a thing were possible. Mac took one look at the dead alien bodies and for a moment he seemed to go into an eye-rolling trance. Mac then opened his eyes, and calmly told Clem they were called the Delp.

I asked him, "How could you possibly know that?"

When I glanced over at Clem, he had no reaction at all to what Mac had just said. Something was happening here, and I felt like the last person to know. Clem then simply said, "You guys are coming with me." Mac and I proceeded into a sterilization shower, and then we were given white robes to wear. We were deep underground in this top-secret facility. Mac and I were taken into a sterile room with chairs in the center facing each other. Mac was excited, and seemed somehow to know what was going to happen next. I was clueless and a bit scared. Clem entered the room wearing his robe.

I think I said to Clem, "I take it we're not getting massages?"

"You wish" he calmly replied.

In walked three aliens of varying races. One was the same kind we'd seen from the crashed saucer, the ones Mac called the Delp. The Delp were short, stocky and grey-tinted, with elliptical eyes. The Delp seemed to look right through you. The Zera were a foot taller than the Delp, but they still only stood five feet tall. The Zera had a striking resemblance to the faces on the Easter Island statues. I came to view the Zera as quiet and somber. The final race was the Rell. The Rell were six feet tall; they looked humanoid with Asian-looking eyes. My mind was racing with questions, but I was afraid to ask them. I turned to Clem and said, "What now?"

Clem said to me, "Prepare to get the worst headache of your life." Just as Clem finished saying that, an intense pain began in my head. It was like ten elves with hammers banging my brain for about thirty seconds.

Suddenly, the pain stopped. I heard a voice in my head asking, "How are you feeling?" At that moment, I made eye contact with the alien called a Rell. Clearly, he was the one asking the question, using some form of telepathy. I answered him with thought, not voice. It was amazing. Somehow I was given the ability to communicate in this way.

I was also able to hear Clem's thoughts at the same time. I laughed as I listened to Clem thinking to himself. I clearly heard Clem say, "My fucking head is killing me." As a scientist, I viewed what I was involved in as a once-in-ten-lifetime's experience. The Rell looked at Mac and seemed nervous. Using thought only, I asked the Rell why he was scared. He hesitated before answering, but then messaged that he was concerned because he could not hear Mac's thoughts. I looked at Mac, who was waiting for something to happen. Apparently, Mac had not had the short-term headache that Clem and I experienced, and was not in mental contact with these aliens. Clearly, all of these three aliens were concerned that they weren't able to penetrate Mac's thoughts.

The next thought I heard was from the small grey Delp: "Why are we bothering with these primitive hosts?" The Rell tried to calm the Delp's emotions, while the Zera just sat there stone-faced. Clem sent me a mental message that we had to leave soon; after ten minutes the headache would return. Obviously, these sessions had a ten-minute time limit.

My final question at this first meeting was directed to the Rell, as he clearly was the most receptive. I asked, "How long have these alien races been visiting Earth?"

The Rell's answer was immediate. "Since before you walked upright. We have followed the hosts since inception." Suddenly our heads hurt again, and Clem said aloud that it was time for us to go. We returned to a much higher level inside the underground facility for a debriefing. Apparently, Clem had had many previous meetings with the various alien races, and filled us in with great detail. Mac was more convinced than ever that his new "gift," as he called it, was directly related to these alien species. He wasn't sure how just yet, but Mac was certain that he was to have a key involvement with what these aliens wanted on Earth.

Clem then told us, under a "national security, keep your mouths shut or else" disclaimer, what the alien races had asked of him. Clem said after the crash of the Delp saucer, the aliens revealed themselves. The Rell spoke as the group leader. The aliens offered to share technology with us, openly, offering guidance in both science and medicine. In return the Rell asked to be allowed to experiment, from time to time, on humans and animals. The Rell said their human experiments were strictly related to DNA and brain function, and that no humans would be killed or permanently injured. Clem said President Truman agreed to the terms, mostly because we had no way to stop them from doing whatever they wanted to do anyway.

This was when the stories of alien abductions truly began to accelerate. People were taken in their sleep and returned before dawn, that sort of thing. I asked Clem why they referred to humans as "hosts." Clem said that was his main question as well, and he hoped I could help him find the answers. Clem admitted that his mind wasn't as open as mine was, and that he felt I'd be able to get many more answers from the Rell ambassador than he could. I asked Clem to try to set up a one-on-one meeting with me and the Rell ambassador. I wrote a list of questions which I needed to get answers to within that ten-minute time frame. The next morning shed much light for all of us.

I was alone with the Rell representative. The meeting that took place was friendly and open on both sides. All of these questions took place in thought. I first asked why he referred to humans as "hosts." Apparently this meant our physical bodies, which contained our souls. I then said that the Zera representative looked like the faces on Easter Island, and in Bolivia and Peru at the ancient sites of Tiahuanaco and Puca Pucara. The Rell smiled when I said this. He said the Zera have been coming to Earth for 20,000 years. They like to build monuments to themselves. With that sentence, I was told that the Rell thought the other races were too self-serving. I had heard the impatience from the Delp, and asked why they were so short-tempered with us. "Some view your kind as lower life forms." Another informative answer.

My last question that day, before my ten-minute window was up, was why Mac had frightened him a day earlier. "We could not read his mind. This is most unusual. The Delp feared that he might be in contact with the Defenders, though I view this as highly unlikely."

"The Defenders?" I asked.

"They are a master race whom we are working for. They have not shown themselves on Earth for countless centuries, as far as we know."

Over the coming months I came to like this alien ambassador from the planet Rell. I usually asked for any meeting I was a part of to be just the two of us. I didn't like or trust the Delp, and the ambassador from Zera wasn't at ease around Mac. Plus, we both felt that the Zera didn't have anything to say at these meetings, so why should we include them? What I did find out over those months was that the Zera was the race that had put the face on Mars, mostly, as the Rell would say, "for selfish reasons." Stonehenge was built by the Rell. It was supposed to be an astronomical map, but the Rell never finished it. I had asked about the DNA testing that the aliens wanted to do on humans and why it was necessary. I was told that the pollutants in the air and water required some gene-sequencing so the human bodies would have a fighting chance to fight off serious diseases. I didn't fully believe this explanation, but I did not let the Rell ambassador know it at the time.

What I found most fascinating was the way the aliens could slip in and out of our dimension as easily as we entered another room in our homes. I was never able to find out more from the Rell ambassador regarding this other dimension they all lived in. I was told that this dimension was outside of space-time. Meanwhile, Mac had set up a one-on-one meeting with the Delp, without my knowledge. There was something about those little grey aliens I mistrusted. However, once Mac got up a head of steam to do something, he was hard to talk down. Apparently, at Mac's "secret" meeting, he felt the discussion was a success because the Delp offered to show him their spacecraft. Mac's excitement level dropped a bit when Clem told him that he would have given him the same tour.

Mac also told me that the Delp had agreed to take us for a ride in their ship. I asked Clem if the aliens had ever taken him for a ride. He simply said, "Yeah, I got fucking nauseous and told them to take me back. But don't let me discourage ya." I felt a little less nervous about taking this flight after Clem said that he had done it. Clearly, I would have preferred the Rell to take us for this ride, not the Delp, but I was committed at this point. When we boarded the spacecraft, a cigar-shaped, orange vessel, I didn't like the look the two Delp pilots gave each other before takeoff. I mentioned it to Mac, and as usual he blew me off, thinking I was a paranoid worrywart.

What I was not aware of before take-off was that Mac had bragged to the Delp that he was in constant contact with the Defenders. When Mac mentioned this to me as we raced into space, I got five times more nervous. The Delp said nothing to us, mentally or verbally, on this trip. Mac couldn't hear their thoughts, and frankly, I wasn't upset to skip the pounding headache necessary to communicate with them. The ride itself was amazing. It seemed like the ship took a series of 90-degree turns to slingshot us from point to point in space. I would have enjoyed the ride much more if I hadn't been thinking I'd be dead in five minutes. We passed Venus, and then turned around and headed into what I later found out was called the Argus Cluster.

We returned to Earth about four hours after when we left. The cloaking technology allowed us to pass through Earth's scanning devices without being noticed. The Delp pilots almost seemed to be snickering at us when we left the ship. The alien races could use language or the written word to communicate; the Delp had done neither on our trip. Mac was able to establish contact with the Delp using handwritten notes at his previous meetings, which helped set up this flight. As we disembarked Mac was excited, but I felt something was wrong.

CHAPTER 23

THE DEFENDER

I was extremely nauseous when we landed, throwing up for over an hour. Mac was sick as well. We both drank water to keep from getting too dehydrated. I felt a strong urge to get away from these aliens for awhile and return to my apartment in New York to rest. I explained to Clem that I needed some time off to think about things. Clem didn't have a problem with Mac and me leaving for a time. Clem said the Rell ambassador had given him a device to contact them if we needed to speak. Mac also was tired, and wanted to go back to New York with me to rest and talk about what we had seen.

When we finally made it back to my apartment, I felt one hundred years old. We dropped our suitcases and Mac almost immediately fell asleep on the chair in my living room. I moved to the kitchen to make a peanut butter and jelly sandwich, and as I began to eat it, a glowing white light appeared in my living room. In thirty seconds or so, this light turned into human form. Suddenly, a naked man was standing in my living room staring at me. He appeared to be forty years old. Before he spoke to me, this alien realized he had no clothes on, and copied the clothes I was wearing with a whisk of his hand.

The alien in human form then spoke to me. "You'll have to excuse me; it has been several thousand years since I took this form. I should have remembered the clothes."

"Who are you?"

"I believe that the alien visitors to your world refer to us as the Defenders." I wanted Mac to see this, so I asked the Defender if I should wake him.

"Let him sleep for now. It is you I wish to speak with at the moment. The Delp have played an evil trick on the two of you. I can assure you that they will be punished."

I asked the Defender exactly what the Delp had done to us. The Defender then opened his hand to reveal a round metallic ball of some kind.

"The Delp took you through a sponge field. It's an extremely deadly area of space for humans, due to the high levels of radiation. This radiation belt drastically increases the aging process in humans. If I did not intervene, you and your sleeping friend over there would both be in another dimensional plane by morning."

"Dead? Can you prevent this?" I asked hopefully.

The Defender walked over to me and handed me the metallic ball. He told me to just hold on to it for a few minutes. "The sphere will reverse the radiation-induced aging. In a few minutes, give it to your fellow time traveler." I was shocked that he knew we were time travelers, but then again, with what had been happening to us lately, nothing surprised me that much anymore. I then walked to a mirror in the hallway and saw my hair turn from grey to black, the wrinkles in my face disappear, and the color in my face strengthen.

"You'll be fine now. Give it to your friend; he is starting to look a bit crusty."

I then put the sphere into Mac's sleeping hand. "You two have had a very interesting life. All of us in soul services owe you a debt of gratitude for succeeding in changing this planet's history."

"Don't mention it," I said. Suddenly, I felt more confident and asked the Defender a few questions. I asked him if he had anything to do with Mac's ability to speak to the souls of the dead. As he looked at Mac peacefully sleeping and looking younger by the second, he responded with an affirmative nod. Mac was right; this was all somehow tied together, and Mac and I were center stage.

Before Mac awakened, I asked the Defender what his job on Earth was. He told me that he was one of twelve Defenders that roamed the known galaxies. Earth was within his quadrant of space to patrol. Because of the population boom to come, he had enlisted three alien races to assist in the collection, holding, and dispersal of souls on Earth and on other humanoid planets. The Defender was here, primarily to trap the Delp, and possibly the Zera as well, in a soul-hoarding scheme. I wished that Mac was awake, because this was more his area of expertise.

The Defender explained that souls are returned to Earth every 350 years on average. However, there were exceptions. If you lived a good life and were killed prematurely, you might be brought back sooner. Or, on the other hand, if you led an evil life on Earth, you might be condemned to come back as a snake for a thousand lifetimes before moving up the evolutionary scale. Every person has God-given talents and weaknesses. Those that can utilize their strengths and protect their weaknesses usually do well in this life. Just before Mac awoke, I asked the Defender if he believed in God. The Defender smiled and said, "Of course. We all report to someone."

The Defender then said he wanted Mac and me to help him trap the Delp. Apparently, some galactic law prevented him from punishing the Delp directly. I asked the Defender how they influenced humans on Earth. "Some call us your conscience or your alter ego. Every human has a soul and an advisory alter ego. It helps guide humans through life."

Suddenly, a 500-page document appeared on my kitchen table. "Look this over; find any loopholes we can use against the Delp in our legal agreement with them."

"I'm no lawyer," I said. The Defender told me that he would help us when dealing with the other aliens, and to have no fear.

I asked the Defender if he had anything to do with us traveling back in time. He seemed pleasantly surprised by my question. "Let's say that we put the idea in your friend's head"—he pointed to Mac, sleeping in the chair—"that changing history was possible. The physical act had to be done by humans; in that we could have no involvement."

Continuing, I then asked if DNA-testing of humans was really necessary. The Defender agreed with my intonation within the question itself. He said it was not necessary, and was in fact a violation of their agreement with the Delp, Rell, and Zera. My last question was why the Defender had given Mac this ability to hear the souls of the dead. "Honestly, it was simply to create suspicion amongst the alien races in the hope that they would trip themselves up somehow," he said. "Not being able to read Mac's mind would frighten some of them." How the Defender knew how to manipulate future events together to reach a positive conclusion that would come about only many years later was truly amazing to me.

The Defender explained that when his kind come to Earth they prefer to use a different form. As Mac was awakening, the last thing the Defender said to me was, "Our thoughts will be tied together, and you will know what needs to be done when you look into my eyes." At that moment, the Defender turned into a dog, a black mutt, sitting in the middle of my living room.

As Mac awoke, the metallic ball rolled out of his hand, off his lap and onto the floor, rolling towards me. I picked up the ball and asked Mac how he was feeling. He said he felt great, and he thought I looked good, too. Then Mac noticed the dog sitting on the floor. "Hey, where'd you get the mutt? He's a cute little fella." He got up to pet him. I laughed when Mac asked me if he missed anything while he was sleeping. I casually told Mac the Defender came and gave him a 500-page book to read. Mac got so excited, he ran to the kitchen table to start reading. I looked at the dog and he barked once. It seemed like a private joke between me and the canine Defender. Mac asked what the dog's name was. I said, "Let's call him Defender."

Mac loved that idea. "Yeah, that'll shake those Delp up."

I'm not sure if it was my idea or the Defender's, but not telling Mac that the dog was the Defender made things interesting. Mac loved petting him, and I just hoped that the Defender didn't mind, as he didn't seem to. The funniest thing happened the next morning, or maybe it was afternoon; I think we each slept 16 hours that night. When we woke up, the "dog" was sitting on the couch. Mac grabbed the book the Defender had asked us to read and sat down next to the dog. I was really enjoying the fact that I knew the dog was an alien with incredible power and insight, while Mac just thought he was a cute pooch. Mac asked me if we should walk the dog. I looked at our four-legged friend at the same time Mac did, and the Defender just shook his head NO. "Wow what a smart dog," Mac said at that moment. He didn't know the half of it.

Mac kept asking himself questions aloud as he read the book. Then the dog would bark once and make eye contact with Mac. Moments later Mac was answering his own questions, thinking he had figured out the answers himself. I was laughing so hard and trying to hold it in. I had to leave the room a few times. The Defender in canine-form did have dominion over humans in this way. It was truly fascinating. I shouldn't have been laughing so hard, as my turn would come in this game as well.

One example I can recall was when Mac asked the question, "Why would the Delp and the other alien races need access to the dimension of the dead?" Then after looking into the dog's eyes, he said, "Of course! To get access to the pool of souls waiting for a new form, and their turn for the next life. They could then illegally appropriate souls and sell them in the galactic black market."

The doorbell rang late that afternoon. It was Clem. He had come to see how we were doing. Our Rell friends were concerned that the Delp may have harmed us, so Clem flew to New York to make sure we were okay. He had become a great friend. Mac was anxious to read the book in private, so he left after Clem came over and headed for the public library to read in peace. I then tried to explain to Clem that this dog was really the Defender the other aliens feared. He didn't fully believe me, so I had him look into the dog's eyes.

"Holy crap," Clem exclaimed after this short session. Then the dog jumped on the table and looked into my eyes. Clem saw me trance out as he had when looking into the Defender's puppy brown eyes. When I came out of it, I had been given a mission by the Defender. Leaving the dog behind in my apartment, I told Clem to come with me, and then I grabbed the metallic sphere and left my building. As Clem walked with me he had more energy in his step than I had ever seen him have before. "I can't believe that dog is one of those Defenders the other aliens fear so much. Where are we going, anyway?"

I was heading for New York Hospital, room 321. As we got off the elevator on the third floor, I instinctively knew where room 321 was; how, I still don't know. Clem was as eloquent as ever, asking, "What the fuck are we doing here?" A doctor spoke to me somberly outside of room 321, saying that he wished there was something he could do, that the boy inside this room was terminal.

As we stood outside room 321, nurses were running in and out of the room at a frantic pace. Inside the room was a twelve-year-old Russian boy named Victor. He was encased in a plastic bubble. Clem asked another of the doctors what was wrong with him. It seems that a gene defect caused normal sunlight to give this poor child radiation poisoning from just walking in daylight. The boy had leukemia, and was only hours from death. His attractive mother sat at his bedside with a handkerchief to her face. I entered the room and reached under the plastic bubble, placing the sphere in the boy's hand. I grabbed the mother's hand and said he would be all right. Next, I told Clem I was hungry and we went for lunch.

I told Clem over lunch that the Defender first came to me in human form, before turning into a dog. I also told him that he gave me that metallic ball to absorb the radiation in our bodies and return us to health. Clem said, "Okay, the dog told you to come to the hospital and give that metal ball to the kid?" I told him yes. As Clem picked up the lunch check he said, "First I run into you guys with ray guns from the future. Then I'm talking to aliens from other planets. And now dogs are telling us what to do. Did I miss anything?"

"No, that should cover it for now."

When we returned to the hospital room less than an hour later, the nurses were smiling and happy and doctors were staring at their charts at the foot of the bed, arguing over which one of them had cured the boy. I walked into the room alone. The bubble had been taken down, the boy was awake, and his mother looked at me with angelic eyes. As I moved to the side of the bed, I made eye contact with the boy. He spoke to me in Russian, which his mother translated for me. The boy had said, "I knew you would come." That comment alone didn't shock me that much, but when he added that the Defender told the boy that I would bring a metal ball to save his life, that did catch my interest.

Even Clem, standing in the doorway, heard the boy say "Defender". Meanwhile, the boy's mother was thanking me in broken English and offering herself to me, I think. I thanked her for the offer but told her that wasn't necessary. My attention was on the boy. I then asked the mother to translate for me. I asked the young man when the Defender had told him this. The boy said in his sleep. With all the things that had been going on, this made perfect sense to me. Clem walked over to the Russian mother and spoke with her for a few minutes. The boy handed me the metallic ball and smiled.

Clem and I went back to my apartment. The dog was nowhere to be found, but Mac returned shortly after we did. Mac and I hadn't even unpacked from our last trip out to Groom Lake, and now we were off again. Mac said he found a few clauses to threaten the Delp with, while reading the 500-page alien agreement. When the three of us got to the airport, the Defender dog was sitting there waiting for us at the gate. Clem and I knew that the dog was the Defender but Mac did not, which made for a very humorous flight. Mac kept raving about how smart "Defender" was, and he was amazed that the dog knew we were going to the airport. Clem just kept saying, "Smart freaking dog, all right."

A steward at the gate came over and said that the dog could not fly with us, but had to be boxed up and put in a cargo hold. Defender then jumped on my lap and stared up into the eyes of this steward. As two other men came over to take the dog away, the steward turned to them and said, "It's all right—this dog has clearance." The dog even got his own seat. I wondered to myself why the Defender dog was traveling with us. I figured that he could have just shown up at Groom Lake or wherever/whenever he wanted to. As it turned out, the dog had a plan. All three of us were given certain telepathic powers that would help us deal with the aliens when we arrived. We each looked into the Defender's eyes at various points on the trip and assimilated information that he wanted us to know.

Mac was beginning to suspect this was no ordinary dog. We were taken to the secret facility, went through the sterilizing shower, and entered the room where we met with the Delp, Zera, and Rell. There were nine of us present and ready to begin—two of each species of alien, Mac, Clem, and me. Then, in walked the dog. Defender sat directly on Mac's lap. As I recall, Mac was petting him right up to the point Defender turned back into human form. Anyway, first I accused the Delp of trying to kill us by taking Mac and me through a sponge field two days earlier. Then Mac blurted out something from the 500-page agreement, that the Delp and Zera were guilty of hoarding souls and not dispatching them in a timely fashion. Clem just sat with his hands holding his muscled biceps, looking angry. I later called it the Mr. Clean position.

The best part of this meeting was that Clem and I didn't get the headache that accompanied the telepathic interface from our previous sessions. We were all able to hear each of the alien's thoughts, and once they realized this, all six aliens seemed much more nervous. The aliens feared the dog too, and protested his being in the room, but Clem just said, "The dog stays." Even Mac was now able to hear the alien thoughts, though they could not read his. Mac said that the Delp and Zera would be banished for 1,000 years for what they had done.

Clem and I looked quizzically at Mac for saying that, but we noticed that he was glancing into Defender's eyes before he said it. The Delp spoke first, when they said they were testing Mac's word that we were in touch with the Defenders, by taking us through the sponge field. "Obviously, you may have been telling the truth." At that moment the dog jumped off Mac's lap onto the floor and assumed human form, this time with clothes on. The look on Mac's face was priceless.

The Defender simply said that the Zera and Delp have been in violation of a 4,000-year-old agreement, and that both the Zera and Delp would be banished for 1,000 years from entry into this dimension. At this point, the always-quiet Zera spoke up in English stating that it was the Delp who had come up with this plan to hide souls for future use, and that they had never participated in this conspiracy. The Defender smiled, said nothing, and then stared at the two Delp aliens for a moment. The Delp began to shake violently, and then they disappeared.

The Defender then said, "The Delp have been returned to another dimension for a period of 1,000 years, whereupon a review will take place for reinstatement for trans-dimensional travel. As to the Zera, view this as a final warning: there is to be no further testing of humans for DNA alterations or anything else. And finally, stop taking advantage of lesser technological societies by having stone figures built in your image."

The Defender looked at me and smiled when he said that line. The Zera and Rell then gladly disappeared on their own.

Mac addressed the Defender: "I hope you didn't mind all the petting." The Defender had a great sense of humor; he simply said Mac was an excellent petter. I asked the Defender why we had to read that 500-page document since it didn't seem pertinent to what went on in this room.

The Defender agreed with me, and said, "One of the other alien races had to implicate another for any action to be taken. When the Zera accused the Delp, the case was made. I had a feeling that Mac would agitate them enough to get the Zera to give up the Delp."

There we were; the Rell and the Zera had left Earth, not likely to return anytime soon, and the Delp had been banished to another dimension. It was just the four of us in the room now. Mac asked the Defender if his ability to hear the souls of the dead was to be taken from him. The Defender asked Mac if he wanted this "gift" to continue or not. Thinking a moment, Mac said, "If it's okay with you, I'd like to keep the gift and help people trying to reach loved ones on the other side." The Defender told Mac that he would allow him to retain this ability for now, but that he shouldn't abuse it. Mac was never sure what that meant.

I thanked the Defender for saving my life and Mac's with the sphere. He nodded but did not respond verbally. Clem sheepishly asked the Defender, "Ah, anything you want me to do?"

The Defender looked at Clem and said, "Look after your time-traveling friends." Finally, the Defender said to us all, "It is time to for me to go. Your service to this planet's future shall not be forgotten in the generations to come. Farewell for now."

The Defender then turned into energy and disappeared. At this moment, Clem turned to us and said, "I don't know about you guys, but I need a few stiff drinks."

Clem stayed at Groom Lake and asked Mac to stay in Nevada for a few more days, which I found a strange request. Before I left for the airport to travel back to New York, Clem said there was a surprise waiting for me at home. Despite my request for more details, Clem would not say anymore about it. When I got back to my building, to my surprise, the Russian boy Victor, and his mother Svetlana, were in my apartment. This was no doubt Clem's surprise, and why he wanted Mac to stay in Nevada. Clem had apparently given Svetlana Kartov the keys to my apartment when they spoke in Victor's hospital room. Clem overheard her say that she wanted to thank me. I had no idea how to proceed here. All that I was looking forward to was a restful evening after a long flight. This turned out to be quite different.

Actually, Svetlana sensed my nervousness regarding the situation at hand, so at first she offered to make me some dinner. My refrigerator had never been so full. Svetlana and Victor had been living in my apartment for two days and she had time to go food shopping. I agreed to have her make me dinner as I unpacked my bags. When I went into my bedroom Victor was fast asleep in my bed. I decided to leave the bag and unpack later. When I walked into my second bedroom, Svetlana's clothes were strewn about, and I did notice a very sexy teddy on the bed.

Over a dinner of steak and potatoes, I tried to tell Svetlana that all of this wasn't necessary. I told her that she didn't have to clean and cook for me, or do anything else, alluding to the teddy on the bed. Svetlana would have none of it; she just said "eat."

After dinner we had some small talk, and when Svetlana realized that I was not going to take the lead here, she took me by the hand and walked me to her bedroom.

Wow, she was amazing. What an incredible night! The morning was a bit awkward though. Victor walked into the room where both Svetlana and I were under the covers. The boy smiled and said something in Russian, which Svetlana translated for me. "My mother sleeping with an angel. Wait until daddy finds out that you slept with an angel. He will be so happy."

My Russian wasn't very good, but I did hear the word "daddy" in there somewhere. Svetlana told me that her husband was in Moscow. In a very matter-of-fact manner, Svetlana got dressed and slowly packed her bags to leave. She turned to me before leaving and said, "I could not repay you in rubles for saving my son's life, so I give you pleasure. I told my husband that I could not return to Russia until I thank you. Last night I thank you, now I can go home." Svetlana and Victor were gone within the hour. Again, I thought back to that expression about women needing a reason to have sex. That was the only one-night stand of my life.

The interwoven aspects of this entire adventure in time amazed me. This young man who was saved by the sphere the Defender had given me, turned out to be an ancestor of my friend of the same name in the future. The Defender's telling me that he put the idea in Mac's head about going back in time to change history. All of it just seemed like a fairytale, but in fact, the threads of this galactic quilt were intricately woven.

It was now the early 1950s, and Mac was leaving for Switzerland to become a clairvoyant. I had no doubt that given the Defender's blessing, he would become world-renowned for his abilities. There was one funny incident the day Mac was leaving. As we walked down a Manhattan street, we saw a black dog with a red bandana around his neck walking toward us. The dog was weaving his way through the crowd. Mac and I froze in place as the dog approached us. Mac turned and commented, "This is a sign that I'm going to be successful as a clairvoyant."

As Mac finished talking we heard a woman yelling and running after her dog. She caught up to it right in front of us.

She picked her dog up saying that, "Poopsie was a bad girl." I still laugh when I think about that incident.

I told Mac I'd see him in three months. He needed time to buy a house and settle into his new home, surroundings, and job. The three months I spent before going to see Mac in Switzerland were truly annoying. First the FBI came to see me: they had some incomplete report on "my activities" and were trying to find out what I had been doing. I bullshitted them pretty well, (as Clem had told me to do if they came calling). Then someone from Naval Intelligence came to see me. America had fragmented into five or six varying intelligence agencies and it became clear that none of these agencies ever spoke to each other. I became very impatient listening to the same questions flying at me from the alphabet soup, which was my name for American Intelligence.

CHAPTER 24

MAC THE ALL-KNOWING

At last, I was just a few days away from my flight to see Mac, and there was a knock on my door. It was Louise. She had tied up her "loose ends" in Europe and came to see me. Louise seemed a bit distant, but to be honest, I really didn't know her that well. I felt that 90 percent of her life was still a mystery to me, yet I wanted to be with her in the worst way. I asked Louise if she wanted to join me on my trip to see Mac in Basel, Switzerland. She told me to go by myself because she had business in Washington, anyway. We spent two great nights together, and then off I went to see Mac.

In ninety days, Mac had accomplished some amazing things. He lived in a two hundred-year-old mansion, with servants. The servants were all young women with dresses that barely reached their thighs. As I waited at the front door for Mac to let me in, a feeling of foreboding came over me. The feeling left me quickly, but I had to acknowledge its presence. Mac then came to the door wearing a smoking jacket and slippers, smoking a pipe. My first impression was that Mac was really playing this role to the hilt. He was thrilled to see me, gave me a tour of his house, and showed me his special séance room, with crystal ball and all.

Mac sensed that I thought he was over the top, so he toned the rhetoric down a bit. I knew that his talent was genuine, and I was anxious to see him at work. That very evening a young man was coming over with an amazing story. I was asked to sit in. The young man was a nice quiet boy in his early twenties. His problem was that his father had recently died of a heart attack and didn't tell his son where their money was hidden. The young man's mother had passed away years ago; there were no brothers or sisters. According to this young man, the father had promised to tell him where his money was hidden, and then he died suddenly. Apparently, the father did not trust banks.

Before I forget: one thing that amused me was that Mac's maids all called him "The All-Knowing." To hear them say it over and over became a bit much. Anyway, during the séance Mac did not need to hold hands or any of that nonsense, as he called it. Mac would fold his hands in front of him, and call out for the boy's father by name and then ask the father to speak through him. Moments later, Mac then said quite calmly, "Neal, you wished to speak with me?" The boy asked his father where he had hidden the family's money. I was fascinated by this.

The father was speaking through Mac. "Yes, that's right; I dropped dead before I told you. Okay, remember the lake we went to on your fourteenth birthday? Do you also remember the rock on the road where you broke your ankle?" The boy kept saying yes to his father's questions. "Thirty feet north of that rock is where I buried all the money. Don't spend it all at once; think about your future and save money. Most important, don't be an idiot like your cousin." With that, Mac came out of it, not remembering anything of what he had just said. Mac then said to the young man, "That'll be 1,000 francs." The boy paid it gladly. I think that he was going to find a lot more money than that. The young man had made a great deal but Mac didn't mind; he loved using his gift to help people. He was so happy doing what he was doing, and I was happy for him.

In the coming days I saw Mac help the police find a missing body, and then a lost dog. Mac even solved an open murder case simply by asking the dead man who had killed him. The police went on to build a case around the suspect, and when they gathered some admissible evidence, the man was arrested. Mac was the go-to man in Switzerland for unsolved crimes. One night after dinner, the foreboding feeling I'd had previously returned.

I remember saying to Mac that something just didn't feel right to me. Mac asked if I had become a seer, too. Suddenly, only a few moments later, a man shot his way into Mac's home. Neither of us had ever seen this man before. He said that before he killed us, he was to tell us that "Hillman gives his regards." I asked this man how he had found us. He removed a tracking device from his pocket; Mac and I then realized that we had never removed our transponders from our bodies. I thought we would both be dead in seconds, and we probably would have been, if another man, whom we also had never seen before, hadn't thrown the door open and killed the assassin.

As we sat dumbfounded, this second man said, "I don't know what this means, but Clem Rizzoli promised the Defender that he'd keep an eye on both of you."

Mac and I were in shock, happy, and in a mood to toast Clem Rizzoli. We even invited the agent sent to protect us for a drink. Clem had been having Hillman followed in Brazil. It would seem that Hillman hired this assassin to kill Mac and me. The agent having the drink with us told me that he was on the same plane as the man he just killed. He then followed him to Mac's home. We made sure to get this man's address for our Christmas list. Mac even told him that future generations of his progeny would be blessed because of what he had done for us this evening.

The agent helped clean up the scene, and took the body for disposal. We didn't ask where he was taking it. After the agent left, Mac asked me how I knew that trouble was near. It was strange because I seemed to have developed a sixth sense of sorts, perhaps from my mental contact with the Defender. Mac and I went to a local surgeon whom he had helped recently in one of his crossover meetings. The surgeon was able to remove our transponders from behind our right shoulders without much difficulty. Mac and I did not want a repeat of this incident to happen anytime soon.

The next morning at breakfast, Mac kept talking about the average person returning to a new body every six generations. However, if you died heroically in combat or to save others, you could return in forty years. If a person had led an exceptional life, that soul would only be returned to Earth by choice, having the option to move to a higher plane of existence. Those rare individuals would have their souls kept under Defender control, not under the Rell or Zera. Mac was getting into such detail that my head hurt like it did when I met the aliens at Groom Lake.

To get Mac onto another subject, any subject, so my head wouldn't explode, I asked him if we could contact Kartov in one of his séances. Mac became immediately fascinated by this idea. That evening with windows wide open, Mac attempted to contact the soul of Victor Kartov, our good friend. It took longer than usual for Mac to establish contact, perhaps five minutes or so, and then a cool breeze blew into the room. It was my job to ask Victor questions, so when Mac said, "Congratulations on a successful mission," I told Victor that we couldn't have done it without him. I then asked how he was killed. "We were retreating into a village outside of Stalingrad. Because of my leg injury I was unable to keep up, and a sniper shot me in the back."

My last question was where he was now, and what his soul was doing. Mac chuckled before answering, "There are rules, Jeff. We can't share everything from this dimension with you. I will say that many of us have jobs to do and individuals in the dimension of the living to watch over. Others in this realm just sleep until they are placed in another body. It depends on the level of consciousness a soul had reached in their last lifetime. Jeff, by the way, thanks for saving my great grandfather's life. It is time for me to say goodbye. I wish you both long lives." Mac came out of his trance and told me that he was able to hear everything Victor said through him, and that had never happened to him before.

I enjoyed my time with Mac in Switzerland, and part of me wanted to stay and be Dr. Watson to Mac's Sherlock Holmes. However, I did not feel that this was my final destination in this timeline. I decided to return to New York, hoping Louise was still nearby. I told Mac to hire a bodyguard because Hillman might know where he lived now. Mac agreed. It was hard to leave Mac, but I had to move on.

CHAPTER 25

DINNER AT THE RIZZOLI'S

When I got back to my apartment, Louise had left a note saying that she would stop by to see if I was home three days later. I called Clem to thank him and to give him the details of what had happened, but he already knew, because the agent had told him. Clem was coming back to his New York home for the weekend, and he invited me to dinner Friday night, adding that I should bring Louise. I thought to myself that Louise in the Rizzoli household would be an interesting mix of English etiquette and Brooklyn foul language. I had to accept.

Louise came back Thursday evening in an excellent mood. I had learned not to ask too many questions about what she was doing. She agreed to the dinner plan at the Rizzoli's the following evening. I wish I had taped it. Clem's family was in full form, even as they attempted to be more polite than usual, and I think that attempt lasted about five minutes. Clem's wife yelled out to a son upstairs to "Clean your fucking room." Louise raised an eyebrow, but showed no more emotion than that.

When Clem's wife asked Louise if we were going to get married, this made Louise a bit more uncomfortable than the foul language. "We'll see," was Louise's response, but Kathy Rizzoli did not like that answer and she let Louise know it.

"Hey, sweetheart, either you're just screwing the guy or you're serious and want to get married. Which is it?" Before

Louise could come up with a response, Clem told his wife to mind her own fucking business.

When we left, Louise said to me on Clem's front porch, "I had no idea people like that existed." Louise and I never married, but we did see each other several times a year. As the years passed from the early 1950s into the late 1950s, I had taken up painting and actually had a very relaxing decade. Clem called me in 1956 to tell me that Eisenhower and the Rell had had a face-to-face meeting, which I found interesting. No further details of the meeting were given to me, but this seemed most unusual. I was curious what they might have discussed.

CHAPTER 26
PRESENT-DAY MAGIC

At this point in Jeff's life story, I noticed that he was very tired, and it was past 4 a.m. I told Jeff that he could continue the story the next day after a good night's sleep. I quickly set up our guest room with new sheets and we each slept until noon of New Year's Day. We were both a bit hungover when we woke up, so I made a big pot of coffee. I asked Jeff if he wanted to go to a local diner for breakfast. He agreed immediately. We went to the Blue Bay Diner in Queens, and continued talking over our lox, eggs and onion omelets, which is known in New York parlance as a LEO.

While I was eating breakfast, a thought entered my mind. I asked Jeff if he still had the metallic sphere that saved Victor Kartov's young life. Jeff answered hesitantly that he was still in possession of it. Jeff added that he didn't want any testing of the sphere. I assured him that was not my intent, that all I wanted to do was to see if the properties that neutralized radiation were still active. Jeff wondered what I had in mind. I asked if he wouldn't mind taking a ride with me to Harrisburg, Pennsylvania. As Jeff calmly put it, "I'm yours for the day." After a quick stop at the nursing home to pick up the sphere and a change of clothes, we were off to Harrisburg. I told Jeff that my uncle Frank and several of his colleagues, who had worked on the cleanup of Three Mile Island's 1979 nuclear reactor meltdown, were all ill fifteen years later.

These men were all kept in the basement of a special radiation unit, in complete isolation.

Jeff was curious to see if the orb he carried could help my uncle and these other men. When we got to the hospital, we made our way into the cold basement level where we both picked up a chill. Jeff was shocked that men in this condition were kept in such a cold environment. We then had a humorous moment with the woman Jeff and I called "Nurse Ratchet." She guarded the door to the room my uncle and the other five men were located in.

"Where do you think you're going? This is a restricted area!" The nurse weighed at least 250 pounds and Jeff tried to comically distract her by saying that there was a food cart coming down the hall. Jeff even pointed in the direction of the imaginary food cart. She was not amused. I told the nurse that my uncle was inside and I wanted to see him. The nurse said, "No visitors without two doctors signing off on it." A doctor came over to tell us that no visitors were allowed and that all of the patients were extremely ill from leukemia, caused by radiation poisoning over time.

I figured that was it and we wouldn't get to see my uncle, but Jeff then took out an NSA ID card and said that he had to speak to these men. I was not allowed in, but Jeff was. While I was in the hall for several minutes with the doctor, I asked him the prognosis for the six men inside. He shook his head, "Look, I don't wanna shatter your hopes, but these men are, at best, weeks from death. All of them have received over fifty blood transfusions and their internal organs have been enlarged or compromised. There is nothing anyone can do to save them." At this point Jeff walked out of the room slowly.

Jeff spoke to the doctor in a soft voice, asking him if he had extended any hope for these men? "The men are terminal, I'm *afraid." The doctor said this with great confidence. Moments later, one by one, the men in that room walked, with IV poles in tow, toward us in the hallway. Each man seemed to get stronger with every step.*

Jeff took the metallic ball from his pocket and he said to me, "It was the strangest thing, after the last of the six men held the ball for a few moments, it turned to solid lead." Jeff then turned to the doctor and said, "I guess this throws a monkey wrench into your diagnosis. Don't be so pessimistic next time."

The doctor stood silent and in awe that these men were seemingly healthy again. My uncle Frank and his best friend Peter were asking if there was a Burger King nearby. I would have stayed and talked for hours with my uncle, but felt I had to get Jeff back to Queens. Besides, I wanted to hear the rest of the story of his life. I told my uncle I would call him later that evening to see how he was doing. Before we began the drive back, I called my aunt and told her that her husband was cured and would be coming home. She nearly fainted from the good news. My uncle and his co-workers gave Jeff a tearful hug I will never forget. No words were spoken, but in that one gesture, my uncle and the other men thanked Jeff for saving their lives.

As I drove back to New York, Jeff pondered in amazement at the incredible intertwined nature of life. "I've held onto this sphere for years collecting dust, and then I meet you; tell you a story of my life, which ties into your uncle having radiation sickness, and the fact that my sphere can save his life. No one can tell me that you and I meeting each other was coincidence, young man. The Defender's hand touched us both."

Jeff and I talked about life in today's world on the ride back to Queens. I asked Jeff if there were many medical advances from his previous timeline. "Not that many. Our society did *not cater to the ill, unless they were high party officials or their immediate families. The Nazis were a survival-of-the-fittest bunch." This was New Year's Day, 1994, as I was driving back to New York. On the radio we heard Vice President Al Gore talking about climate change and the inherent dangers of it. I asked Jeff what he thought about climate change.*

Jeff smiled before answering. "Even in my time, there were some who believed that global warming or cooling was a man-made event. It is true that carbon dioxide gases trapped in the atmosphere have an effect on this issue, but whether the Earth is warming or cooling is based on two main factors of nearly equal proportion. The first is the number of humans living on the planet. As that number increases, the planet will warm. The most important factor is sunspot activity. During times of increased sunspots or the lack of them, the planet will either warm or cool. Sunspot activity usually works in 11-year cycles. Earth now has well over six billion people living on it, which is four billion people more than lived in the world I came from.

This was the most informative ride of my life. To be able to hear what Jeff's view of the world was, and the possible ways to improve it, was fascinating. I didn't trust my memory; I prayed that the batteries in my tape recorder were getting all of this. I asked about energy sources from his time. When I asked this question, it was interesting to see how positive Jeff became about the accomplishments of his timeline in this area. "In the mid-twenty-first century there had been an Arab revolt against the Nazis stationed in Saudi Arabia. The moronic Nazi commander ordered a nuclear strike to punish the Arabs involved."

"In a chain reaction oil fire, the entire Middle East went up in smoke and blackened the skies for weeks. The result was that oil became too costly to use as the world's main energy

source. The order went out to advance solar energy, and no price was too great to complete this directive. Five years later the planet was using the most advanced solar panel technology ever conceived. The costs were enormous, but when the Party sends out a call, all scientists know that their lives are at stake if they fail, so innovation happens. So, to answer your question, we used a solar mirror in space to collect the sun's direct energy and then fire that stored energy at seventy different collection points on Earth. All homes were powered in this way. Our cars were electrically powered."

I then asked Jeff what he foresaw for our world that he helped shape. Jeff shook his head in an undecided fashion. "There are so many different possible outcomes to this Earth's future. It depends on the people in power around the world. Clearly, demographics are troubling. There are too many people on the planet, creating too few resources for hundreds of millions of people. This will cause a greater disparity between the richer nations and the poorer ones. I also see that certain cultures are having 8 children per family while others have 1 child per family, which will cause a major shift of world power over time."

When I mentioned religion, Jeff got a little testy. "So many of the Earth's wars were fought in the name of religion. I wish the planet lived by the Ten Commandments and consolidated all religions to that single set of principles. However, I know this will never happen. I wish the Defenders would have stepped in somehow and made that change to our world, but that is not their way. Perhaps, in the future, they will give someone an idea that can turn religious hatred into harmony."

Jeff seemed so drained at this point, I didn't ask any more questions. I just put on some music for the rest of the drive back. Jeff kept commenting on the metallic ball which had turned to lead. "It's as if the Defender knew back in the early

1950s that this one final task needed to be done in 1994, before the sphere had completed its purpose. Don't you ever get the feeling that the future has already happened and only a select few know it?"

I didn't want to touch that question. It sounded too much like Plato from that philosophy course I took in college. When we got back to Queens, I stopped at the nursing home so Jeff could shower and get some new clothes. Jeff had agreed to finish his life story back at my house after dinner, and in case it went deep into the night, he could sleep over again. We went to a famous restaurant specializing in steak. My budget was a little tight, which Jeff noticed by the look on my face when I read the prices on the menu. Jeff smiled and said that he'd take care of the bill.

We were now well-fed and ready to continue where Jeff had left off, when we got back to my house. I opened the last bottle of Borolo, and Jeff continued the tale of his life's amazing journey.

Clem came to see me late in 1956 and asked if I'd mind letting his team of experts dissect my handheld computer for reverse engineering advancements. I think Clem's boss, whoever that may have been, wanted Clem to use our friendship to get more technological knowledge out of me. I agreed to let Clem examine my computer, mainly so he could get brownie points with his boss, and with the caveat that if they broke it, I would get 5 million dollars. Clem laughed and said, "Why not, maybe we can make some money on this deal."

The unit was returned to me seven months later, but it never worked quite right after I got it back. Despite my half-hearted complaint to Clem, we saw no money for our trouble. The last years of the 1950s were quite uneventful for me.

CHAPTER 27

THE SPACE RACE

Clem called me one night in 1959, as the Russians had put Sputnik into orbit. Suddenly, the American space program became a top priority. Knowing that I had experience in rocket propulsion systems from my earlier days in an alternate reality, Clem asked if Mac and I would help America build rockets. I accepted and Mac refused. When I had called Mac in Switzerland he turned me down for two reasons. One, he thought that the rocket program might lead the world closer to a nuclear confrontation, and he didn't want to be a part of that. Mac's second reason was that he loved his life and what he was doing, and didn't want to leave Switzerland.

I moved to Houston, close to the space center. My initial job was working on the Atlas rocket program. Clem had given me another identity, because he felt the FBI or NSA would ask too many questions. That's why I just use the name Jeff. My last name has changed more times than Elizabeth Taylor changed husbands. I later found out that Clem Rizzoli was also a made-up name, though he refused to tell me what his actual born name was. Clem called it a security maneuver to protect one's family from extortionists or kidnappers. I felt this was a touch cloak and dagger, but I understood the reasoning.

After I got to Houston and started working, I was shocked to see so many other German rocket scientists. The Americans and the Russians imported all the German V-2 rocket scientists from the war to fight their space race. I had all the intermix formulas that were needed to safely propel men into space. The trick was to disseminate the information slowly, and to make sure other people got the credit. Clem strongly suggested that I keep a very low profile, or else other agencies might become alerted to my presence.

I worked at the Houston Space Center on special assignment for eight years. In 1963, after John F. Kennedy was assassinated, I had an urge to see Winston Churchill. I needed to hear his reassuring words. Louise came with me to London and Mac flew in from Switzerland. I had seen Mac, on average, twice a year. Usually, it was me going to Europe. Only a few times did Mac return to the United States.

When we met in London, we all had a good time. Winston was older and a bit frail. His mind was as sharp as ever, however, especially when we spoke of the war. Mac and Churchill monopolized the conversation, talking about the occult which, I was surprised to learn, Churchill had an interest in.

We were visiting Churchill's home and speaking in his library, when from the corner of the room I heard, "Screw Hitler, kill the Nazis." Churchill had a large parrot called a macaw that said this over and over again. At first it was funny, but then became a bit tiresome. Churchill said it wasn't his bird, but that a friend had lent it to him. He thought I'd get a kick out of it. Churchill also said he had had an African Grey parrot in the Thirties for a few years, but didn't have the patience for the constant sweeping up.

Mac had been monopolizing Churchill's ear, but when Mac went on the house tour, Louise and I were left alone with him. I asked Winston what he thought would happen in America after the Kennedy assassination. Churchill said, "Why, nothing. The country will mourn the loss and move on. The government won't fall, if that is what you were afraid of." The confidence of Churchill's words was so definitive.

It put me more at ease almost immediately. Then Winston let something slip that made both Louise and me extremely uncomfortable.

Churchill said to me that Louise loved her latest assignment, which was in essence to spy on me and find out anything she could for England. That one sentence caused my feelings for Louise to diminish instantly. Louise was equally uncomfortable; she had trouble making eye contact with me after Churchill said that. Winston caught on, and apologized for leaking something he thought I knew. When Mac returned from his house tour, he knew something had happened between us, but wasn't sure what. I suppose I should have realized that Louise may have had ulterior motives during the time we spent together, but it still hurt me.

I was more numb than angry. I told Louise that I didn't want to see her for awhile, and despite Mac's attempts to talk me out of it, I returned to Houston to bury myself in my work. I stupidly told myself that I did not deserve to be in another relationship in my lifetime, in part because of the family I had left behind in another reality. I said my goodbyes to Winston, having the strong feeling that this would be the last time I would see him alive. At parting, I told Mr. Churchill that, in my opinion, he alone had been the glue of the Allies' fight during the war. Clearly the Americans were the power brokers of the war effort, but it was Winston Churchill who kept that singular focus for our fighting men to follow. As I said this, Winston just rocked in his chair smoking that cigar with a big smile on his face. That is how I will always remember him.

Mac returned to Switzerland, though he did offer to come to Houston with me to make sure I was all right. I told him to stay in Europe. On my return to the Space Center, it was full steam ahead for me working on the Gemini space initiative.

In 1964, I met a young man being given a tour of the facilities. His name was Gene Roddenberry.

Mr. Roddenberry was talking to a colleague seated next to me. I overheard the conversation and was very impressed with the idea Mr. Roddenberry had come up with for his new television series called "Star Trek." There was to be a multinational crew, with an alien from another world as an officer on the bridge. I thought this man was very forward-thinking, especially when you consider that the best science fiction television show of that time was "Lost in Space."

When it was my turn to meet Mr. Roddenberry, he asked me what I specialized in. I'm not sure why I said this, but my response was, "Time travel theory." I suppose I knew the answer would cause the young writer/producer to want to sit down with me and talk. We had lunch for forty minutes and I enjoyed every moment of it. Gene was fascinated with my theories of time and space, and he even took a few notes. Of course he had no idea that these weren't just theories but fact, as I had lived most of them.

Gene was an incredibly insightful man. He said to me that he felt "Star Trek" would give the young people of the world a common future and a voice for unity in an increasingly more difficult world. With the Vietnam War beginning to get deadlier, his words were of hope. I wished him well and of course was an immediate fan of the show. I was very much honored when Mr. Roddenberry offered to pay me to be a science advisor, but I had to turn him down. I was tempted, but made a promise to Clem to keep a low profile. In 1965 Winston Churchill died. I met Mac in London for the church service, and I noticed that Louise was in attendance as well. We exchanged a half-hearted hello. I think Louise was more open to talking about "our issues" than I was at that time, but frankly, I was still not in the mood.

CHAPTER 28

THE KRAZ THREAT

Until 1967 I led a very normal life, by some standards: living alone, going to work for many twelve-hour days, then returning home late at night to eat a TV dinner, watch an hour of television and then going to sleep. This was my routine for almost eight years. This mundane calm preceded the raging storm of bizarre events to come.

Clem came to see me with that familiar look of urgency I had seen before. "Would you come to Colorado with me to look at something?"

I said "Of course," and off we went. On the plane, Clem filled me in. When we reached our destination, the San Luis Valley in southern Colorado, I saw convincing evidence that aliens were back at their old tricks here on Earth. A young colt had been killed by precision laser surgery. The entire head of the horse had been stripped clean of all flesh and muscle, and the brains and all internal organs were missing. There was not a drop of blood at the scene.

No earthly surgeon, even with the Eradicator, could have performed this surgery. Clem knew this too. We just weren't sure how to proceed. In the coming days we were to see literally hundreds of various animals across the countryside mutilated in the same way. I asked Clem what the agreement was that Eisenhower had signed in 1956, and if that agreement allowed the aliens to dissect animals. Clem said he wasn't sure, but he thought not. I then asked if he still had the ability to contact the Rell. He did. We had too many questions; maybe the Rell could give us some answers.

It seemed like déjà vu, but here we were again at Groom Lake, going through the sterilization shower, and then waiting for the Rell in the clean room. While we waited, Clem asked many rhetorical questions. "What the fuck do these guys want with horse brains, cow livers, and pig hearts? I wish the Defender dog was here." What Clem was asking wasn't funny, but the way he said it was. I felt a bit more at ease when the Rell entered.

The Rell was the same one I had met previously. After Clem and I came out of the 30-second intense headache phase, we all could hear each other's thoughts again. Clem asked the Rell almost the identical question he had just asked me. The Rell told us that they were not responsible for the animal mutilations, nor were the Zera or the Delp who had been banished to another dimension. "Then who?" I asked with my mind. The Rell said that a race outside of the Defender arrangement with Earth was gathering information on their own, for purposes they were unwilling to discuss.

Clem was not happy with this development. "Another alien race to deal with? I didn't sign up for this."

I asked the Rell if there was anything he could do to help us in our investigation. All the Rell would telepathically tell us was, "Not at this time." It reminded me of one of those Magic 8 Balls that would give you similar answers to yes-or-no questions. The Rell then slipped into his other dimension, departing after a very unhelpful meeting. Clem was now concerned that he had to make out a full report and didn't have anything conclusive to state to his superiors. I tried to console Clem, then returned to the quarters provided for me in this underground facility.

When I opened the door to my small room, a very familiar black dog was sitting on my bed. The dog quickly turned into the Defender. This time he was wearing clothes. I congratulated him on getting the clothes right this time. (I had gotten to the point where seeing alien races appear and then disappear didn't faze me anymore.) The Defender told me an alien race known as the Kraz were responsible for the animal mutilations, and they were a very dangerous military dictatorship that had annexed many worlds. The Defender said that the Kraz only operated in one dimension: ours. The Defender then told me that he could offer us only very limited help in trying to stop the Kraz from their plan to add the planet Earth to their empire.

I stood in stony silence as the Defender kept talking. I would have said something, but this story was so fantastically frightening I just stood frozen and listened. The Defender continued that he had arranged with the Rell to transport us to the Kraz vessel when we were prepared to do so. "What?" This was all I could say at that moment. The Defender smiled and said that perhaps I should take a shower and refresh myself before he continued.

"The Kraz are testing the organs of animals and people to see if they can assimilate to your planet's atmosphere and the inherent pathogens in the air and water. If they report to their home world that they can adapt to Earth, that would be a very poor assessment for all living beings on your planet. Please focus on what I am telling you. The Rell will get you on board their ship, and then you must find a weakness in their physiology and exploit it. Earth's present inhabitants' only chance is to make certain that the Kraz reject Earth as a suitable planet for them to colonize."

I asked the Defender how the Kraz would conquer Earth if the planet was deemed suitable for them. "In any number of ways: If they were willing to wait 100 years they could simply sterilize all the females on Earth and wait for all of you to die off. I think this less likely, as the Kraz are not a patient race. They would probably attack the planet with a larger version of your Eradicator weapon mounted on their ship in orbit. They could kill hundreds of thousands with each firing of the weapon."

"Let me talk to Clem and see how we want to proceed," I said.

"Very well. I suggest you make your plans quickly; the Kraz are nearly done with their analysis of your world." The Defender disappeared into energy. When I told Clem what had happened, he had me retell the story to two of their smartest scientists at Area 51.

As all involved were devising a plan, Clem said, "We need someone to go with you, someone with special training in espionage and information retrieval." I agreed.

Twenty-four hours later, who showed up but Louise? Clem called her, but did not tell her what the mission was. That was my job. I called Clem "Cupid" after he called Louise for this assignment. The Kraz sounded all too familiar to me, a galactic version of the Nazis I had left behind. Louise knew most of my past, but the alien races we had encountered after the war would come as quite a shock to her. First, Louise and I had to clear the air over our differences in regard to our last meetings. The fact Louise was going through my papers, safe, and who knows what else was hard for me to get over. However, under present circumstances, with the planet's fate at stake, forgiveness came quite easily.

This was Louise's first visit to Area 51, although she told me later she had tried to sneak in on several occasions for British Intelligence. I walked Louise back to my room so I could attempt to discuss what she had volunteered for. This was not going to be easy. Before I could begin, Louise felt she had to apologize for spying on me at various times over the years. She told me she had been conflicted, and almost resigned because of the feelings she had developed for me.

I told her that she was just doing her job. I blamed myself for getting involved emotionally with someone who was clearly distracted and distant. Those kinds of relationships don't usually work out. Then I told Louise, "Let's get this behind us, because we have to be at our best if our mission is to succeed." Louise asked me what the mission was. She went on that she knew we would be working undercover in a dangerous environment. That was all that Clem had told her. "Louise," I said, "Do you know that aliens from other worlds have visited the planet Earth, and some of them can be seen here on this base?"

Louise was 50/50 as to whether she thought I was kidding. "Here, at this base? Aliens from other worlds?" I had great difficulty getting Louise to accept this concept, and just as I was about to give up, there was a strange scratching at my door. As I opened the door, the Defender dog was standing there. Knowing that the next minute would be precious just to watch Louise's reactions, I simply opened the door and sat down.

Louise asked me if this was an alien in the form of a dog. She thought she was kidding, and then the Defender dog became human before her eyes. As he turned from dog to energy and then back to matter in human form, Louise grabbed my arm so hard I thought she'd break it. "Louise, this is the Defender of our quadrant of space and the being in charge of soul dispersal." Louise shook the Defender's hand gently and then fell onto the bed next to me, weak in the knees.

The Defender spoke to Louise specifically on this visit. He told her, "I have shown myself to you because of the seriousness of the situation for all the human inhabitants of this planet. There is a militant alien race known as the Kraz that are going to attempt to take over your world. I would suggest you view them as the Nazis of outer space. I got that analogy from Jeff's mind."

Louise was shocked, but regrouped quickly and wanted more details about who these Kraz were and how they could be stopped. The Defender went on to explain that he would give us both a "unique" ability to understand the Kraz language in their presence. The Defender put his hands gently on our heads. Instantly, we both had the ability to understand any and all languages spoken or written. It was amazing. I asked the Defender why he was willing to help us, but in such a limited fashion. "After all, you could wipe out these Kraz with a single thought."

"Unlike the Delp who were under contract to us for services to be performed, we have had no contact whatsoever with the Kraz Empire. We are aware of them, just as we were aware of the Nazis in your world from the other timeline. The situations are very similar in many ways. We did not interfere directly on Earth and we are bound by the same rules regarding the Kraz. However, since indications are that the Delp may have told the Kraz about Earth's location, I am somewhat culpable here. This is why I am willing to help you at all, in this limited way."

Louise was fascinated by this discussion, although she didn't understand most of it. She wanted to ask questions, but decided to keep listening instead. For the next two days we had meeting after meeting with tactical officers and SWAT teams that were preparing to join us on board the Kraz vessel. As our plan was finally taking shape, our palms got a bit sweaty. The Rell had agreed to transport Louise and me, plus fifteen heavily armed and well-trained Navy Seals, directly onto the Kraz war ship. The Rell agreed to transport all of us back to their ship, exactly three hours later. No matter our condition at the time, all seventeen of us would be brought back to them and then simultaneously transported to the clean room at Groom Lake.

The Rell were completely neutral in this fight, but were helping us because the Defender had asked them to. I was in my late fifties at this point, but felt like a twenty-year-old. The plan on this first trip to the Kraz vessel was to capture one of the crew at the three-hour mark, so he would be transported back to Groom Lake with us. Louise and I were to be accompanied by ten of the armed men to try to get to the computer center, located in the engineering section of their ship, and try to download any information about the Kraz we could find.

The Defender had told me how to obtain this information from the Kraz library banks. We were ready to go. I was scared, but tried to calm down by telling myself that the Defender wouldn't allow anything to happen to me. Whether this was true or not made no difference: it did calm me down. It was the strangest sensation to be transported from the Rellian vessel via a "Star Trek"-like transporter device. It felt like you became a soul with no body for a split second, and then reformed back into matter.

We were transported to an uninhabited spot outside the engineering section of the Kraz ship. As we moved closer to their engineering section, we saw our first crew member. My goodness! He was seven feet tall with a horn coming out of his forehead, dressed in a military uniform made of iron. Or it least it looked like iron. Two of the Seals were able to shoot the Kraz crewman with a silencer loaded with a heavy tranquilizer. As the armed men moved down the corridor slowly, I took out a syringe and drew blood from the Kraz crewman. I was going to take the blood back to the lab at Groom Lake and look for a weakness to exploit.

When the way to engineering was clear, we all made our way inside. I found it strange that there were no guards posted in the engineering section, as there were vital components of the ship located there. Even though the Defender had given Louise and me the ability to understand the Kraz language, the computer was encrypted with such detail I couldn't break their code within the time allotted. All I was able to accomplish in engineering was to remove the chrome chip of the Kraz's Eradicator weapon. The Kraz design for their Eradicator was remarkably similar to the one we had in the alternate reality, but on a much larger scale.

I took out a nickel that was in my pocket; how it got there, I have no idea. I slipped the nickel into the slot the chrome chip had been located in. Both the Kraz chip and the United States currency were the exact same measurement, 7/8 of an inch in diameter and just under 1/8 of an inch thick. The nickel fit like a glove in the slot, and with any luck, the Kraz might take days trying to find out why their Eradicator was malfunctioning. Louise was trying her hand at the computer station, (and she was actually making more progress with the encryption code than I had), when an alarm sounded on the ship.

We were clearly in trouble, as we had no way to get off the Kraz vessel until our three hours were up. I told the head of the Seal team that we should leave the engineering section, because if they knew we had been in there, the Kraz would start looking more closely for signs of sabotage. As we made our way up a hallway, a guard spotted us and a firefight took place. We were all running for our lives, as bullets and laser weapons' fire were flying all around us. Seven of our men were killed; I'm not sure how many of the Kraz crewmen were killed, but several of them were injured as well.

It became apparent that we were surrounded, so I encouraged the mission Commander to surrender, which we did. I told him to stand down; we only had to stay alive for another hour before we'd be transported to the Rellian vessel. Our wounded would also be beamed off the ship. We were briefly taken to a holding cell, and then Louise and I were taken for questioning. I suppose they figured since we weren't in uniform, we may have been the brains of this operation. We were taken to their bridge. Very impressive large screens for tactical use were everywhere on their bridge. The Kraz captain put his hand on Louise's chin, quite gently actually, and said, "Females on a military mission, how strange."

Louise and I both thought the Kraz were speaking English, but moments later we realized that the Defender had given us the ability to hear them in our language, and they heard us in Kraz. The Kraz commander did not understand how we could communicate so easily, but gave us the credit for it. I recall his telling us, "It appears that your world has technology that we were unaware of. So be it, how did you get onto this vessel and why are you here?"

I decided to be honest, up to a point. I told him, "We know that you have gutted hundreds of our cattle and taken all of their internal organs for testing. We had to assume that your intentions were hostile, so we were sent to investigate."

"This does not answer how you have gotten aboard my ship."

"We used an experimental matter/energy device to get aboard." The Kraz captain was uncertain if I was telling the truth. In his indecision he circled around us, and picked up Louise by the throat, lifting her three feet into the air. "You realize, that if I determine that you are lying to me about anything, I will snap her neck like a twig."

"I believe you. Please put her down." He slowly complied with my request. When Louise was safely on the ground, I asked the Kraz captain, "May I ask you why you have come to my planet?"

With no fear of reprisal by the combined military forces on Earth he said, "Because if we deem your world suitable, we will kill 90 percent of your kind and put the survivors to work in the mines to refine ore for the Kraz Empire."

Louise and I went silent with that statement. Although we knew this to be true from our conversation with the Defender, it was still shocking to hear it from this seven-foot tall, ominous-looking giant. I glanced at my watch, and we were just a minute or two from being beamed back to Groom Lake. My mind was racing as I tried to come up with a plan to help Earth's cause. I decided to try to find a way to hold onto the Kraz captain and have him transported back with us. Momentarily, the captain was sidetracked by one of his men asking a question, so I told my idea to Louise, she quickly said, "I'll do it." We checked our watches again, and we had less than twenty seconds to go before we were retrieved by the Rell.

Louise told the Kraz captain that she liked strong males who knew how to take control of a situation. With that, the Kraz captain grabbed Louise by the shoulders in a somewhat passionate embrace. The last thing I heard him say before we were all transported out was, "Let me show a human female what a Kraz male can do." The next thing I knew, we were all on the Rellian vessel, and the captain of the Seal team got the drop on the Kraz commander and took his weapon away.

As the Kraz captain was disarmed, Louise broke her embrace and said "Now you'll see what a human female can do. You are now our prisoner." The Rell used their matter/energy device and sent us all back to Groom Lake. With the Kraz captain in handcuffs and seated at the conference table, Clem began his questioning. This debriefing seemed pointless to me, but Clem felt it needed to be done. I acted as translator, then when I went to the lab, Louise took on that role. Later, Louise and I were in the lab with a team of scientists looking for a physical or biological weakness in these large humanoids.

We were all feeling our way in the dark, as we had never seen blood like this before. The Kraz blood was jet black, like oil. Louise and I knew full well that taking the Kraz leader hostage was a dangerous thing to do. We had no idea how his crewmates would respond, so we knew time was of the essence here. The Kraz blood was able to withstand every sort of radiation we threw at it, and there was no weakness we could find. Next we tried bacteria and viruses, which the Kraz blood fought off with amazing ease. We had to find something soon or our planet would be in grave danger. We knew that there must be some element that the Kraz feared, or they wouldn't be testing our animals and atmosphere so expeditiously.

Suddenly, a helium canister valve burst, and our lab air was filling with helium. Moments later a nitrous oxide canister malfunctioned in the exact same way. Louise and I were now speaking in very high voices from the escaped helium and laughing from the nitrous oxide gas. Louise thought this was quite a coincidence, while I viewed it as the Defender's subtle assistance. Under the influence of the two combined gases, all of the blood cell samples from the Kraz soldier were now dead. We later determined that a ratio of 88 percent helium to 12 percent nitrous oxide would kill, or at least incapacitate, the Kraz. I found it hard to believe that these two seemingly innocent gases, when combined, would kill the black-blooded Kraz, yet those were the facts. We had supposed that the Kraz lung capacity was their weak link, which these two gases negatively affected.

Louise said the funniest thing when we made this discovery. "One good thing for these Nazis from outer space, they'll get to die laughing." Now we had to come up with a plan that would kill the Kraz aboard their warship and, far more importantly, to conceive a plan that would prevent the Kraz Empire from ever wanting to return to Earth. Meanwhile, Mac had just arrived at Groom Lake. I didn't know that Clem had called him, but I was sure glad to see him.

Mac wanted to see the Kraz commander as soon as possible. I wasn't present when Mac walked in to see him, but the story I heard later was that when Mac saw the size of this alien, and the foot-long horn coming out of his forehead, he made an about-face and left. Clem entered the lab to tell us the story of Mac's grand entrance, when his voice got an octave higher, and the laughing gas made the story sound even funnier to all of us. "You guys must be having a blast in here. We need a plan, not a party."

We managed to close off the valves to both gas tanks and then explained what we had found out to Clem. He was very excited that we had come up with a way to kill these aliens, but we needed time to devise a plan. Clem told us that the Kraz were not at all in a negotiating mood, and they no doubt would try to use their Eradicator sooner or later on the human inhabitants of Earth. Clem wanted to use the gas option as a first strike weapon. It was Louise who devised the plan that we decided to use with the help of the Rell, once again.

The plan was extremely dangerous. However, it was the best idea that we could come up within our limited time frame. Louise and five members of the Seal team would return to the Kraz vessel with the proper mixture of helium and nitrous oxide, which would be mounted on the backs of the Seal team specialists. Louise would go back to the engineering section and continue what she had started before the alarm went off on the Kraz vessel. She would try to get into their computer system in order to enter false atmospheric readings of our planet, which would show much higher levels of helium in our atmosphere than are actually present on Earth.

The idea of this plan was to discourage other Kraz warships from entering our star system. Our hope was that other Kraz vessels in space would be able to access this information, and realize Earth was not a suitable planet for their species. Louise would also put in a log entry that the atmosphere was so toxic to the Kraz that this planet should be avoided at all costs. We had no idea if Louise could accomplish any of this, but it sure sounded good to everyone in that situation room.

While Louise and the Special Forces crew were heading back to the Kraz vessel, with the Rell's less-than-enthusiastic assistance, Mac and I had a face-to-face meeting with the Kraz commander. We honestly had no idea what to do with this Kraz captain. Clem then came running into the interrogation room, asking to see me immediately, outside, for a private conversation.

I left Mac alone with a handcuffed Kraz commander, and joined Clem outside the room. Clem told me that the second in command on the Kraz warship was demanding the immediate release of their captain, or they would use their weapon to kill ten million people on Earth. I told Clem we might have some extra time because I switched out the chips in their weapon core. Hopefully it would take the Kraz at least several hours to discover the switch.

Clem contacted Louise and the Seals, who were already aboard the Rell ship ready to take off. Obviously, the urgency had just increased tenfold. Louise and the Seals were all wearing gas masks. The Rell were once again able to transport our team onto the Kraz warship undetected. Once on board, our people made their way back towards engineering. As they began to encounter a few members of the Kraz crew, that was their cue to dispense the gas, which knocked them out quickly as they reached the engineering section of the ship.

Louise was able to break the computer encryption as the Special Forces team stood guard inside the control room within the engineering area. Louise wrote in their computer database that Earth's atmosphere was 17 percent helium and 4 percent nitrous oxide, which was deemed sufficient to make Earth an unlivable planet for the Kraz. Next, she wrote a captain's log entry in the Kraz language. Louise wrote that, "All Earth landing parties were killed after a few minutes on the planet's surface. The atmosphere is toxic to our kind. We recommend no future return missions to this world."

Louise was given a wrist device that she could activate to tell the Rell when she and the Special Forces team were ready to return to their ship. The final job to be done was to send the rest of the gas into the ventilation system of the ship. The men awaited Louise's word for the go-ahead, as she had to relax a security protocol to allow the ventilation system to be rerouted through engineering. Louise mentioned to the Special Forces captain that she didn't know how she could understand the Kraz language so well, and do what she was doing. But as she finished rerouting the command codes, Louise nodded to the men to release the gas shipwide.

The Kraz security forces were on their way to engineering, because they saw suspicious computer activity. Shots were fired, but as soon as the gas reached the corridor of the firefight the Kraz soldiers fell to the ground. Louise activated the recall code and the Rell returned the landing party, unharmed, back to their vessel and then to Earth.

Meanwhile, back on Earth, we were pleading with the Kraz captain to return to his home world and leave us alone. Unfortunately, the reality is that peace can only be attained through strength. The Kraz commander did not think we posed any threat to his world's superior technology, so he laughed at our attempts to placate him. An incredible minute of levity followed, when Mac told me he had a plan. Mac had whispered something to Clem an hour earlier, which at the time I thought nothing of.

Mac left the room and came back in carrying a black dog wearing a red bandana around his neck. This was not the Defender dog; this was an attempted bluff by Mac.

The big hole in Mac's plan was that the Kraz had no idea who or what a Defender was, unlike the other alien species who worked for the Defenders. Anyway, when Mac walked in with this black dog walking five feet behind him, he loudly commanded all of us to "Bow to our supreme leader." Mac got onto the floor on all fours, raising and lowering his hands from the floor to reach for the ceiling. Clem and I played along and we did the same thing. The Kraz commander thought we had all lost our minds, and I didn't disagree with his conclusion. Mac told us to stand, and he picked up the dog and said to the Kraz leader, "Dogs rule our world; that is why we pick up their bowel movements." To me, the funniest thing was that the Kraz commander couldn't understand English, so he had no idea what Mac was saying. I could have translated what Mac was saying to the Kraz commander, but I didn't see the point.

Louise returned to the conference room and stood in the doorway as we were praying on the floor. She said nothing, watching to see what this was all about. Clem got off the floor, walked over to Louise and asked her if everything went all right. She said we were able to do everything we had hoped to do. With that said, Clem walked over to the Kraz leader and asked him, "For the last time, will you leave Earth alone and guarantee that you will never come back?"

The Kraz captain said, "I will see your world destroyed and there is nothing you can do about it." After I finished the translation for Clem, he got very angry.

Clem cocked his head, "I thought you'd say that." Clem pulled out the Eradicator from his pocket and vaporized the Kraz captain. We all stood in shock for a moment, and then Louise began clapping and we all joined in. That was the first time I had actually smiled after someone was eradicated. Clem raised his hands in accepting the applause, then said, "Let's get some lunch." Clem always wanted food after a tough situation was "eradicated."

Clem's final favor he asked of the Rell was to tow the Kraz vessel back into their own space, in the hope that other Kraz military personnel would board the ship and read the computer logs. Deep space telescopes had confirmed that the Rell were keeping their end of the bargain. It was with great satisfaction that I watched the Kraz warship escorted out of our star system, on a viewing screen the Rell had provided. The incident was over. Now that this crisis had passed, we began to look at what was happening on Earth. It was one of the worst years I can recall in this new timeline. Martin Luther King and Bobby Kennedy were assassinated; there were riots in Detroit. The Vietnam War was raging with stories of atrocities. It was a very bad year.

As we tried to figure out our next move, one thing was certain. Louise and I had gotten back our love for each other. Now that she understood everything, our relationship could move forward on an even footing. As for Mac, I really put it to him, as did Clem, regarding the stunt with the dog. "What the fuck were you thinking? We played along, but you had nowhere to go with that." Clem was right, of course, and Mac knew it. I asked Mac if he thought telling the Kraz leader humans sometimes pick up dog excrement would get him to surrender.

Mac got defensive, and said "I didn't see you guys come up with anything else." Maybe you had to be there, but it was funny. I had my doubts about the Rell's sincerity level in helping Earth out of this situation, but clearly, they came through for us here on several levels.

Louise's mental flexibility was amazing; she went from total disbelief in aliens of any kind, to running an operation two days later to rid our planet of a deadly menace. She had an inner strength or reserve able to handle anything that came up. No wonder Churchill respected her so. After this incident all was forgiven between us, and now I had the comfort many American men enjoyed: to be able to come home from work and tell that special someone, with complete truth, what my day was like. Come to think of it, Louise probably looked at me in the same way. We were both lucky to have each other.

As we gathered up our gear and got ready to once again leave the base, Clem came in to talk to Louise and me. It seemed that he was feeling a bit remorseful for eradicating the Kraz commander. I think he wanted reassurances that he had done the right thing. Before Louise or I could answer him, we all received a mental directive of some kind to go to the conference room immediately. Louise, Clem, Mac and I were all walking through the hallways of the base heading for the conference room and we did not know why. Once inside, we all just looked at each other in a mindless gaze.

CHAPTER 29
DEFENDER 11

As we stood there asking each other why we were here, the Defender, in human form, materialized before us. He asked us all to sit down. For the next three hours, the Defender told us the incredible story of his own life, and how he came to be where he was now. Before he began, the Defender addressed Clem, telling him that he shouldn't have any regrets over eradicating the Kraz leader. Clem certainly appreciated the Defender's approval. To further his point, the Defender told us that although he was an egoless, peaceful soul at heart, over the millennia he had been forced by various circumstances to kill millions so he could save billions of life forms.

To make the telling of his story as interesting and memorable as possible, visual images of his experiences were shown on a viewing screen as he spoke to us. It was as if he was narrating the story of his life with a movie of it behind him. The Defender told us he had never done this before, but felt an attachment to all of us, which became clearer as the movie/narration got under way. He caught our attention with his first sentence: "I had a human form, much as yours, some eight hundred thousand years ago. What all of you had to deal with regarding the Kraz warship and the threat to your planet was remarkably similar to what I had to face those many thousands of years ago, in a galaxy 30 million light years from Earth.

"I was the captain of a small five-man starship called Defender 11. There were thirty Defender ships in our fleet.

Our sole purpose was to try to protect the weaker planets from the various military dictatorships that were gaining strength every day. Our arch enemy was known as the Korzellian Empire. These men were very similar in appearance to the Kraz you faced today, but even more powerful. The Korzellians had already taken over ten thousand habitable planets and added their natural resources to the Empire. They set up mining colonies on every planet, and only the fittest of a planet's inhabitants were kept alive to work the mines, so they could build more ships.

"We had only thirty ships; the Korzellians were building thousands. Our numbers were dwindling. Our ships would be attacked by ten Korzellian warships at a time. I received a communiqué from our home planet of Talzon that our world was under attack. My final orders were to blow up a wormhole the Korzellians were using to move between galaxies, to try to prevent their further expansion. This wormhole was well protected, and we had a hell of a time getting to it. We were damaged and unable to destroy the wormhole from our side, so I ordered us to pass through it, in the hope I could destroy it on the other side, wherever that was.

As the Defender told us about his life in human form, the movie that we were watching amazingly moved in tandem with his storytelling. It was riveting for all of us watching it. We couldn't take our eyes off the screen. The Defender continued, "Once inside the wormhole, there were hundreds of different shafts and channels that we could move through. On instinct, our navigator just chose which caverns to enter. When we finally emerged into real space again, we had traveled three hundred light years to an area in space devoid of many stars. We were clearly at the very edge of the galaxy we were now in. We did not detect any Korzellian ships, which was not all that surprising, since there were so many different currents inside the wormhole which could have taken us to one thousand different locations in space.

"Our tachyon power grid was 90 percent depleted when we emerged from the wormhole. Our first priority was to find a planet which had this element present so we could recharge our power systems. Long-range scans showed a possible planet several light years away. We barely reached this world in time; our energy grid was running on fumes.

"The world we had reached was much as your planet Earth is today. There were three hundred different countries speaking a thousand different languages. We were fortunate that our home world implanted universal language chips in the brains of all deep-space Defender personnel. Thousands of known languages were downloaded into us. We were able to speak all of the planet's languages, and understand when these languages were spoken to us. Louise and Jeff, I have given you this gift as well. This was how you were able to understand the Kraz language and their computer language.

"I decided that the five of us on board should go to the planet's largest city. We landed our ship in a remote area outside of this highly populated metropolis. Our engineer needed raw materials to get our tachyon grid to charge properly, so we had to acquire local currency. Fortunately, we had confiscated rare gems from a Zarian pirate ship in our galaxy and were able to trade these precious stones for local currency. We were very fortunate that the humanoid inhabitants of this world looked very similar to us. All we had to do was add a brow ridge to our foreheads to look like the local inhabitants of the planet.

"Within thirty-six hours after landing our spacecraft on this world, we had sold the precious stones to become what on Earth you'd call millionaires. We moved into a penthouse apartment on the most expensive street in the city. I was amazed at how quickly the five of us were able to assimilate into this culture. We were buying television sets, computers, furniture, all the comforts of home. Our engineer bought and built the tachyon collector within days, and we returned to our ship to install it. We had the help of a local boy and his mother to get around. We didn't know how to drive their vehicle properly, so they assisted us.

"When we got back to the ship to install the tachyon grid, long-range scanners showed a vessel entering the system. When we determined that the configuration of this ship was Korzellian, we left the planet to engage them. The Korzellian ship had minimal power as well, as it became obvious that the wormhole had drained their systems, too. We were only able to garner enough energy to fire our plasma cannon weapon one time, but that was enough to destroy the Korzellian warship.

"We had determined that there was no entrance to the wormhole from this side, so we couldn't stop future Korzellian ships from coming through. I decided that we would live the rest of our lives on this new world and try to protect them from the Korzellians. We had a big advantage, because our tachyon grid would be fully charged while theirs would be at minimal power, which would allow us to destroy them more easily.

"My people were happy here on this new world, and we lived out the rest of our lives in relative peace. We did destroy six or seven Korzellian ships over the years, and had to dodge local law enforcement officials from time to time, but we defended the planet well. When I was about 120 Earth years old, my body was nearing its end. I was visited by an immortal being called a Time Guardian, who asked me if I wanted to join a galactic organization to protect time and space. I told him that I would have loved to fifty years ago, but it was a little late for me. He smiled and said, 'We don't need your body, just your spirit.' He then told me that at the time of my passing, I would be joining them in a new realm.

"After I died, my spirit did indeed live on and grow stronger by the day. I was given certain responsibilities of lesser scale, and when those tasks had been done successfully the jobs I was given became more difficult. Over time, I advanced to the position I have attained now.

At this moment, the lights in the room brightened and we had a brief question-and-answer period before the Defender left Earth. I asked the Defender if he had ever been to Earth before, and if so, for what reason? He said that he had touched Mac's mind by giving him the formula to complete the time machine calculations he was working on. "I prefer to do my work on Earth as an alter ego or as conscience. Do you ever wonder where your ideas come from? Sometimes they come from us, or others that work for us, or the souls of the dead whose job, in between bodies, is to guide the living.

Clem asked a good question next. "Who are these Time Guardians, and do you work for them?"

"At the beginning, yes, I worked for them. However, over time, and the ever-expanding Universe, we had to spread out and were given different responsibilities. I was one of twelve Defenders given a territory to patrol in space. The twelve Time Guardians regulate the much more specific task of time travel. Time travel is indeed possible, as you in this room well know. The Time Guardians review every case of attempted time travel, and have the ability and power to stop and reverse the effects of time travel on a given world. In the case of Earth, I cleared what we were attempting with them beforehand, so you need not worry about the Time Guardians' approval.

Mac asked the Defender if he had touched the minds of any other humans with his ideas, as he had done to Mac in the future. "Yes. Scientists, mostly. In the early 1500s I took Copernicus on an orbital ride around the Earth. I made it seem to him that he was dreaming, yet he sensed it was real. He then developed a Sun-centered theory of the solar system, as opposed to the belief prevalent at the time that the Earth was the center of the Universe. From time to time I'd nudge a scientific truth into the consciousness of the living to help in the understanding of the way things truly are.

"I may have helped Hubble in 1923 realize that the Milky Way galaxy wasn't the only galaxy in the cosmos. I just pointed him in the right direction of an expanding universe. As I said, it is easier for me to touch the mind of a scientist, as generally, they are open to new ideas and concepts. Your world reminds me so much of the one where I lived out my years in human form. I feel very close to all of you in my spirit. Your handling of the Kraz situation was very well done indeed.

I then spoke out, "Thanks to your popping the valves on the helium and the nitrous oxide."

The Defender smiled and nodded to me. "Good luck to all of you. Use the gifts I have left you with wisely. Something tells me you will all have more chances to use them. Your world that you all helped shape will go through difficult times and good times in the next one hundred years. Never get too optimistic or too pessimistic; the wheel always turns. Farewell." The Defender turned into energy and disappeared.

We all sat in a momentary silence, until Clem broke the ice. "What the fuck did I get? He got the ability to hear dead people" (here he looked at Mac), "you two can understand and read all languages" (Louise and I), "and I'm left here to write a top secret report that no one will ever read."

Mac put his arm around Clem and told him, "Maybe it's like a baseball trade; the Defender will give you future considerations." I thought Mac's comment might be upsetting to Clem, but he seemed to like the analogy. As depressing as the world seemed outside in 1968, we all felt better about the future as we sat in that room.

I asked Louise to move in with me in Houston, and she surprised me by agreeing to do so. I stayed at the Houston Space Center until after the landing on the moon. Once Neil Armstrong touched down, that was my opportunity to try something else with the rest of my life. To be perfectly honest, after everything that we had gone through at the secret base in Nevada, working at the space center was a bit of a letdown in terms of the excitement level. I was proud, however, to have played a small part in the success of the Gemini and Apollo missions.

CHAPTER 30

MOVING BACK TO NEW YORK CITY

In 1970, Louise and I moved back to New York. I was happy that I didn't have to counterfeit any more money in those years. The salary that I was paid was sufficient to cover our expenses. Louise and I both went through a bit of a depression in the first months of 1970. It looked like our best and most exciting days were behind us. One day we woke up and realized we had been given an incredible gift of language understanding in both voice and print, so we should figure out a way to take advantage of this talent. The Defender wouldn't have wanted it any other way. Next, we had to decide how to employ this gift for language. At first, to test our skills, we went to Central Park and prevented arguments.

The one thing great about living in New York City was the diversity of people. Within a ten-block radius of where we lived were Chinese, Russians, French, Germans, you name it. I called New York City Noah's Ark for this reason. Anyway, we tested our skills on the street, speaking the same language as the people we met. We tried to stop fights between husbands and wives, or business partners, whomever we encountered. At first we irritated people more than we helped them, but we got better at it over time.

Louise then suggested we become interpreters at the United Nations. Neither of us could stand up to the background checks that would have to be done to get us jobs at the UN, so we called Clem and he got us through the approval process. Clem was very surprised that this was what we wanted to do. Clem called the United Nations "The mother-in-law society." Clem felt, and rightly so, that most nations just like to come to the UN to complain about their poverty level or another country's lack of interest in helping them.

Working at the United Nations building in New York at first felt very prestigious, and Louise and I were proud to be using our talents as interpreters. Of course, everything that we would do from now on would be quite a letdown from the exciting things we had been involved with in the recent past. Yet we felt good about working for a worldwide organization. Most interpreters used machines to hear the words spoken, and then translate for the ambassadors via the earphones. Louise and I just sat next to the U.S. ambassador and whispered in his ear what was being said; in this way, he had no need to wear the headphones. This was short-lived, however, as other ambassadors complained that the United States had some form of advanced method of interpretation and demanded either they get the same advancements, or that they be taken away.

Everyone wanted an even playing field, so on that level the complaining made some sense, but this was the beginning of the disenchantment that Louise and I felt for this organization. Louise was bored. She loved the action that her chosen profession had taken her to. I sensed she wasn't long for the United Nations work. One morning the phone rang. Louise answered it and spoke for several minutes. I was still half asleep. When I had gotten my two cups of coffee working, I asked Louise who had called. She said it was her sister in London. I didn't even know she had a sister. I knew so little about Louise, really.

I didn't know what her sister said over the phone, but Louise had a spring in her step that morning. She was clearly looking forward to going to work. I assumed that her sister had given Louise good news of some kind, but I knew not to ask, as I probably wouldn't get the truth anyway. At the UN, I noticed that Louise was acting very friendly towards the Russian ambassador. I was too naive about these things to put two and two together. I was, in many ways, the absent-minded professor. Louise told me she wasn't feeling well, and went to a room at the United Nations where she could lie down and have some privacy.

At home later that evening, Louise seemed distant. I had to ask her questions two or three times before she even heard them. I assumed that she was mad at me, perhaps because I made her repeat things too. You see, I made Louise repeat questions almost daily, as my mind is usually in a constant state of distraction. She hated having to repeat herself, and now it was my turn. As usual, when it came to trying to figure Louise out, I was completely wrong in my assessment of everything happening since that phone call from her sister.

I noticed a little earpiece in Louise's right ear. I asked her about it, and she shushed me. Louise was writing something down on one of those large yellow lined pads, and then asked me to call Clem immediately. Still in the dark, I did as Louise asked. I called Clem and handed the phone to Louise. Louise began reading off latitude and longitude coordinates to Clem, and a time and day. I think she said Friday morning at 0800. She then mentioned the name of a Russian submarine, and finally I was waking up to the reality of the situation.

After Louise hung up the phone, she explained everything to me. It wasn't her sister who called (though she did have a sister); it was Clem. Evidently, there were Russian submarines bringing in parts for ballistic missiles to Cuba. This was a much more subtle version of the Cuban missile crisis, but a potential threat to be sure. Clem had asked Louise to plant a bug on the Russian ambassador, and then listen to his conversations over the course of the day and night to try to find out exactly when the next submarine was due into port in Cuba. She had just heard what she needed to hear when Louise had me call Clem.

Two days later, three U.S. battleships were waiting for the Russian sub. President Nixon called Brezhnev and the Russians backed down, and began removing these missile parts from Cuban soil. Louise was happy to help and get back in "the game," as she called it. I had fallen in love with a woman who needed dangerous activity to feel good about herself.

Despite all of the secrets that I had to keep in my life, Louise now knew 100 percent of my background at this point, while I knew less than 50 percent of hers. I asked Louise about this sister in London I had just heard about, and asked her sarcastically, "If there are any other surprises I should know about?"

Louise looked me in the eye, quite seriously, and said, "Okay, you want full disclosure, here it is. I also have a twelve-year-old daughter who is living with my sister in London."

My first reaction was the typical male response to a statement like this. "Am I the father?"

Louise laughed. "No, you are not the father. Because of the life I have chosen, my sister agreed to bring up my daughter as her own. My daughter calls me Aunt Louise." Louise got very sad after telling me this. I just held her on the couch for an hour or so with my arm around her shoulder. I never did ask who the father was.

The next day I urged Louise to go to London and tell her daughter the truth, but even as I said the words, I wasn't sure this was the best advice. All I knew was that it troubled

Louise to be called "Aunt" by her daughter. Louise said she'd play it by ear and see if an opportunity for full disclosure with her daughter was possible. I told her to take as much time as she needed. Louise left for London the next morning. We had both just resigned our jobs at the United Nations, so we needed to find something else to pique our interest.

CHAPTER 31

Using My Gift

A few days after Louise left, I read a strange story in a super-market tabloid while waiting on line to buy my two-for-one Breyer's ice cream on sale. I had time to read the story only because the woman in front of me was trying to use twenty-five expired coupons, and the line didn't move. Anyway, the article was about a thirty-five-year-old woman in upstate New York, near the town of Genesee, who awakened from a coma speaking an unknown language. I certainly had the time to investigate this, and since the Defender had given me this talent for the understanding of any language I heard, I figured that I could help this woman and her family try to cope with this frustrating reality.

The drive upstate took forever, as I seemed to find every road construction crew eating lunch while closing lanes on the New York State Thruway. When I finally arrived, it was nine hours after I had left New York City. I went to the hospital mentioned in the article, but the woman had been sent home that morning. I had to use an NSA ID to get any information about where this woman lived. By the time I got to her house, it was early evening.

A very tired-looking man who appeared to be in his late thirties answered the door with a look of hopelessness on his face. I was going to use my NSA credentials to gain entry, but after looking into this man's eyes, I decided to tell a more truthful tale. I simply told him that I might be able to help his wife. He looked at me and, mustering his last ounce of hope, let me into his home. When I got to their bedroom, I was shocked to see the woman handcuffed to the bed posts with two clergymen throwing holy water all over the place, in a misguided attempt at an exorcism.

I could understand why the priests thought the woman was possessed, but when you have advanced knowledge that others do not, science may have the answers that religion is slow to believe. The poor woman was scared to death, and with good reason. As she began to speak frantically in a language unknown on Earth, somehow I was able to understand her and respond to her. She was convinced that she was in her planet's version of hell. She understood that the body she inhabited was not her own; whatever form her species took was nothing like we looked on Earth. Fortunately, I had packed a small medical bag, and gave this woman a sedative by injection. I then told the priests to take off her handcuffs.

The priests reluctantly complied with my request to remove the handcuffs, and they were even less enthusiastic when I told them to wait outside the room. The husband saw that I was able to understand what his wife was saying, so he reiterated my request for the priests to leave the room. I used the man's telephone to call Clem. The husband was standing there next to me while I spoke to Clem, but I didn't care what he might overhear. I told Clem to tell the Rell I would be bringing a woman to Groom Lake whom they might be able to help. Clem wanted to know what to say to the Rell when he contacted them. "Tell them there was a mix-up in soul services!"

The husband drove us to a local airfield and we received a special government clearance for a nonstop small jet flight to Nevada. It was an interesting flight. I couldn't tell the husband too much, but at the same time I kept his wife in a half-drugged state so I could ask her questions on the airplane.

When the husband, whose name was Bill, asked me what I thought was wrong with his wife, Rita, I couldn't tell him what I knew to be true. Somehow, this woman's soul had been exchanged with another life form halfway across the galaxy. I simply told the husband we had an experimental drug in Nevada that might return his wife's state of mind. At least we had a fighting chance.

While the husband napped on the plane, I asked the young lady to tell me about her world. Speaking slowly, in a half-drunk slur, she said that there were 300,000 people on her planet, and that her world was at war with another planet in their own star system. I asked her what the last thing was that she remembered. Thinking a moment, she said "giving birth." Then Bill started to wake, and that was all I would ask her for the time being. As the plane landed, Clem came out to meet me at the airfield.

Clem was half laughing when he told me, "Alien shit has really hit the fan!" I asked Clem what that meant. Clem told the Rell what I had told him, and they went searching the galaxy for the soul of the Earth woman. Clem thought the Rell were nervous that the Defenders would do something to them if they failed to resolve this crisis. When we got back inside the base, the Rell had already brought in the body of the alien female who the Rell felt contained the soul of the human woman.

Before attempting to switch the souls back into their proper bodies, the Rell spoke out, saying that, due to the lack of available soul collectors after the Defenders threw the Delp out of this work, mix-ups were inevitable. The Rell went on to say that the Earth woman had mentally given up the fight to save her own body, which also led to this switch of souls. Clem told the Rell, "Okay, now that you got the disclaimers out of the way, do what you came here to do." I looked at the alien body the Rell had brought from another star system. She appeared similar to a centaur from mythology, half woman and half horse.

Rita's soul had never regained consciousness in this body, so fortunately, she never experienced the reality of inhabiting a body that was half horse. The Rell were successful in the transfer, which took a little over an hour. I went to talk to Bill, who was several rooms away and under guard. I told him the treatment had worked, and his wife would be back to normal. I also told Bill that this was a top-secret project and he could tell no one about it. I think this man would have agreed to anything at that point, just to know that he would get his wife back in her right mind.

When I took Bill in to see his wife, as she came out of this transfer of consciousness, she gently grabbed her husband's hand and softly told him she had had the strangest dream. As the husband looked at me and smiled . . . well, life didn't get any better than that. Days later I read a story in an upstate New York paper that said, "Experimental Drug Works to Cure Woman's Acute Paranoia."

CHAPTER 32

VICTORIA

I actually considered spending the rest of my life looking for these bizarre cases around the world and trying to help them. I figured I needed some time to myself first, to give that idea more thought. When I got back to New York, there was a note on the kitchen table from Louise: she had returned the night before and was out shopping. This news made me feel great. Despite her many mysterious trips to Europe, and her various secret agent endeavors, I loved being in her company. Looking around my apartment, I noticed that our second bedroom had a suitcase on the bed, with clothes laid out alongside it.

Honestly, despite my eyes seeing something unusual, my mind didn't register anything I had seen as out of the ordinary. Louise came back an hour later carrying shopping bags of food. As I helped carry the bags to the kitchen, she was happier than I had ever seen her before. Louise told me that she had told her daughter the truth: that she was indeed her mother and not the twelve-year-old girl's aunt. Louise said her daughter, whose name was Victoria, was actually thrilled to hear this news, and wanted to live with her back in New York. Being the oblivious person I am, I said, "No problem, have her come and stay with us." With that, in walked Victoria from the hallway, carrying a bag of food and a smile.

I was no match for those two. They had obviously planned this whole entrance, figuring out exactly what I would say. No matter; this young girl was a great joy to have around, and I

159

relished every moment we spent together. Victoria was a miniature version of Louise in so many ways. She was constantly curious, at times devious, but with that cute English accent that seemed to make you forgive her any transgression.

I didn't want Victoria to swelter in the summer heat, so the day after she moved in with us, I decided to clean out the second bedroom's air conditioner, which had not been turned on in many years. When I got inside the unit, I stirred up a nest of hornets that had made a home for themselves in my previously dormant air conditioner. Two of them landed on my right kneecap and stung me. I was wearing shorts, so this was a direct sting to the body. At that moment, I learned of a bizarre talent that Victoria had acquired. I noticed that Victoria always wore several thick rubber bands on her wrists at all times, and now I found out why. Victoria took aim at the four or five hornets that got into the bedroom. She shot each hornet with one shot of her rubber bands. She didn't miss.

I thanked Victoria for saving me from several more potential stings. She told me not to worry, that she was just doing her job, and then she casually left the room. I found out something else that day. My knees were both mildly arthritic and slightly swollen. The right knee, which had absorbed two hornet stings, was feeling much better, as the swelling went down considerably. I contacted a colleague from Houston who had a hobby of holistic medicine experimentation, and told him what I had discovered. A year later he came out with some sort of bee venom to reduce swelling. It's funny how science works at times.

Having a twelve-year-old girl in the apartment took some getting used to. After getting to know Victoria better, it was clear to me that she was twelve going on twenty-five. I remember being ganged up on regarding the book *Frankenstein*. They both felt that Mary Shelley was the writer of this book, and it was a great work of fiction. I half-agreed with them. I also felt *Frankenstein* was a great book of fiction; however, I was positive Mary Shelley did not write it. I had read most of the works by her husband Percy B. Shelley, the poet and author. The style of writing was exactly the same in all of Percy's writings, as it was in *Frankenstein*. I had postulated that for tax reasons, Percy Shelley authored *Frankenstein* and put his wife's name to it. Well, Louise and Victoria at first thought I was a chauvinist, until I convinced them to read Percy's works and then compare styles. After they read a few of his works the girls never mentioned it again, which I took as a victory. I knew they were both too prideful to ever say I was right and they were wrong.

We had Russian neighbors whom I affectionately nick-named the "Battling Russians." My goodness, how these two would scream at each other. Thankfully they never came to blows, but the yelling was very unnerving. One day the yelling turned into a scream, and Victoria took it upon herself to knock on their door. There was a water-bug crawling on their wall, and rather than kill it, the battling Russians just argued over who should call the exterminator. Victoria ended the crisis with her rubber band, killing the large cockroach with a single shot. There was a new sheriff in town! The Russians were much quieter after that.

We did the usual touristy stuff, taking Victoria to the Empire State Building's observation deck on the 86th floor. I thought she would be a little scared being up that high, but it was just the opposite, "I'd love to hang glide from here." Fearless child. Next we went to the Statue of Liberty; the quote from this locale was simply, "Freedom is worth fighting for."

We capped this long day off with a trip to Chinatown for dinner. Victoria was shocked that Louise and I spoke Chinese and were able to solve a dispute between store owners regarding garbage-can placement outside their establish-ments. Louise wanted to be honest with Victoria, so she told her daughter the two of us had the ability to understand and speak any language on Earth. I was thankful Louise stopped at this point. I really didn't think telling a twelve-year-old about aliens from outer space would be helpful.

Victoria got excited about this gift that her mother and I had, and thought she might inherit this ability somehow. Clem was back in New York, and he invited the three of us over for dinner. I thought this would be quite a culture clash for Victoria to meet undisciplined children her age. I was anxious to see her reaction to this dinner. We got to Clem's house at 6:30, and it didn't take long for the foul language to fly. After graciously introducing Victoria to everyone, Clem's wife Kathy yelled from the kitchen to Clem in the living room, "Are you fucking retarded? You bought the wrong tomato sauce!" Clem politely excused himself and went to the kitchen, where the four-letter words were flying on all sides.

I looked to see Victoria's reaction, and she was smiling from ear to ear. Later that evening, Victoria commented that she liked Americans because they said what they felt. She quite logically thought this healthier than the English way of holding everything inside. During dinner, Clem was a bit surprised when Victoria proudly told everyone Louise and I spoke all languages. Clem just looked at me and raised an eyebrow.

After dinner, we were smoking cigars on Clem's porch when he asked me, "What else did you tell the kid?" I told him that was all, not to worry. Clem then disclosed some unnerving news: Hillman had disappeared and the man Clem had following him in Brazil was dead. Now we were all on alert. I was worried, but my main concern was for Mac, because

Hillman might know where he lived. I called Mac. He was not happy about this development, but he had just hired another bodyguard to make him feel more at ease.

I didn't want Louise to find out about Hillman. I was afraid that she would risk her own life to find him, just to protect me. I felt a distraction was needed, so I agreed to one of Victoria's requests to get a dog. We went to the North Shore Animal League on Long Island to look for puppies. Louise was surprised I had agreed to this, as my stand in the past was that New York City was no place to bring up a dog. As we walked around looking at those cute little faces begging for us to take them home, Louise and I almost froze in our tracks when we spotted a puppy version of the Defender dog. We convinced Victoria to choose this puppy, and of course we called him Defender.

We all loved this dog, and the feeling was mutual. Defender was smart and, as his name implied, he would defend the three of against all of those evil UPS drivers when they rang our bell. I still had to do a double take every time I looked into the dog's eyes; it was uncanny how much he looked like the alien friend who had taken canine form. Louise invited her sister to New York to visit us. I was anxious to meet the woman who had brought up Victoria and done such a great job of it. Victoria agreed to double up with her aunt when she arrived in town.

Louise's sister Pam was a delight to have around. She was a few years older than Louise, and almost a complete opposite to the feisty woman who kept me on my toes. Pam stayed with us for three weeks, and the time really flew by. For a time in the 1970s I felt more relaxed than at any other time in my life. I had that feeling of togetherness I had missed so much from the family I had left behind in the future. Louise, Pam,

Victoria and I all decided to vacation in Europe together, and Mac would join us. The five of us had a great time traveling together. Mac and Pam seemed to hit it off, too, which added an interesting component to this trip. We seemed to find the same free-spirited, long-haired, tie-dyed kids wherever we traveled in Europe. Louise had to explain an expression we heard often while traveling in Amsterdam, "Hey, man, do you know where we could find some weed?" Mac was the person young people usually asked this question of. He was much more in tune on the subject. I thought they were looking for dandelions; Mac knew better. I gave everyone quite a laugh as we walked through Vondel Park in Amsterdam, where many of these kids slept at night. I heard a man say what I thought was "Buy some goat shit?" It turned out he was saying, "Buy some good shit." I'm afraid Victoria thought me a total dork after this latest misinterpretation.

Every few days, Mac or I thought we saw someone who looked like Hillman. We were obviously not at ease, even as we had such a good time going from city to city. We all used the Eurail Pass system, which was great for traveling through Europe by train. It was on these trains that Mac and I thought we saw Hillman.

Mac made the suggestion that we all split up. He said he needed my help on a project. Louise didn't buy it, but agreed nonetheless. Louise, Victoria, and Pam would return to London and await our return. After the girls left, I asked Mac what it was he needed my help on. Mac said he thought he saw Hillman and wanted to get the girls out of harm's way.

CHAPTER 33

The Asylum

Mac did have an idea for our next course of action. He mentioned a small asylum outside of the Black Forest area of Germany that housed six people. "The interesting thing about these six people is that they speak dead languages." Mac felt that between our two talents, we might be able to help these people. I was certainly up for this challenge. We made our way back into Germany, which brought back memories and made me feel uneasy.

Mac was driving and holding a map while he tried to keep us from killing a cow on the roadside. I kept offering to drive; I told Mac that after all we had been through, it would be a shame to lose our lives this way. As usual, Mac thought I was needlessly worrying, "Just because I drove off the road once or twice." Thankfully, after I grabbed the map from Mac's hands, we were able to locate the small townhouse where these troubled people lived. Working with the six people housed there proved to be a fascinating experience.

We were allowed entry without difficulty, and then the owners of the home allowed us to mingle with the people there. We spent nearly four days with these individuals. We determined that three of the six people were just insane. The languages that they spoke were not a language, just gibberish, and they were beyond earthly help by either of us. The other three people, Mac believed, had some triggering event in their lives that allowed them to remember a distant past life.

There were two men and one woman that we examined. The first man, named Fritz, spoke Etruscan, an ancient lost language spoken in Italy. I was ready to punch Mac in the nose because of his constant interruptions when I was attempting to speak to Fritz about his life. Mac kept saying, "What did he say?" I must have given him one of those looks Ralph Kramden gave Norton when he wanted him to leave, because Mac finally kept his mouth shut. Fritz said he was a cobbler from ancient Rome and he didn't know why he was here. From the things he described to me, I'd say he was from around 200 BC.

I felt for this man. There was nothing we could do to help him, other than try to assimilate him to our time. I took off my shoes to show him how shoes were made today. When Fritz showed an interest in the modern shoe, I took him by horseback to a local shoe store. One of the nurses said he would only travel by horse. Fritz was deathly afraid of cars, which was understandable. Now that the people running the small asylum knew that Fritz was a cobbler from 2,200 years ago, they were able to give him shoes to fix. This would at least give him some peace in this life.

The woman was speaking Sanskrit, a language of ancient India. She was not as fearful of her surroundings as Fritz was, but wanted to know what had happened to her family. Her name was Joma, and she was so happy to speak with me for the simple reason that I understood her language.

Joma was calm and remarkably serene for someone who thought she was living in the equivalent of 1000 BC. I had heard of some religious Hindus in India who spoke Sanskrit and were trying to keep the language alive. I asked the people running this house to contact someone in India involved in this religious circle. I was certain that they would like to have a person who spoke this language fluently to study up close.

When the Germans running this small asylum cried poverty, Mac and I agreed to print up some German marks for them. I think we spent a few hours in the car making them a hundred thousand Deutschmarks.

After our generous "donation" to the owners of the house, and their promise to help these three people as best they could, I then examined the third person more closely. This man spoke Aramaic, the language of Christ, and his story was by far the most fascinating. He told me that he had been inducted into Spartacus' slave-army rebellion against Rome. He was a slave from Pompeii whom Spartacus freed on his way to the sea. Mac interjected himself into this interview and used me as his interpreter. This was a reversal of roles for us. Mac asked this man if he was killed in battle. The man looked at Mac and said he thought he had been wounded. Mac turned to me and said the man died in that battle, because the voices in Mac's head were telling him this.

I asked Mac how this man's soul had found his way into this body. Mac got angry with the Delp, blaming them for another mix-up. We found out that Fritz had been hit by lightning, which somehow triggered his previous life episode. Joma was in a coma after childbirth, and when she emerged, she was speaking Sanskrit and remembering a life from 1000 BC. Then there was Kelso, the man from Spartacus's slave army around the time of Christ's birth. Kelso had been in an automobile accident and suffered the worst kind of concussion. Kelso was only unconscious for a day, but began speaking Aramaic when he returned to consciousness.

Kelso had been a manservant to a wealthy Roman family. He never left the house since being sent here, and he had no interest to do so. Kelso was content watching television, eating his three meals and then going to sleep. I asked Kelso what he thought of television. He simply said it was a gift to him from the gods. Mac and I weren't worried about Kelso; he had adapted to his modern surroundings with religion which was, to my way of thinking, the best use of religious belief I had seen in my lifetime.

As Mac and I said goodbye to our three new friends and the people running this home, we felt elated. The Defender would have been proud of the way we were able to use the gifts he had given us to help others. But, as Jerry Garcia once sang, "When life looks like easy street, there is danger at your door." Mac and I had driven just a few miles from the asylum when our car was run off the road, and we crashed in a ditch. Mac was furious at the driver of the other car, and as we got out of the car to give him a piece of our mind, there stood Hillman and two other men, holding guns on us.

CHAPTER 34

HILLMAN RETURNS

My initial reaction was that I was glad Mac had told the girls to head back to London. Apparently, we *had* seen Hillman on that train. After a brief hello, Hillman ordered us into his black Mercedes. We were driven to a large home with a laboratory in the cellar. It was like déjà vu for me, as I flashed back to World War Two in Hillman's underground lab in Berlin. This time the laboratory was in Stuttgart. Mac was more frightened than I was. I wanted finality to this chase through time, one way or the other, and as fate would have it, this situation would not resolve itself without collateral damage.

Hillman had been planning this for over thirty years, or so he said. Before he fled to Brazil at the war's end, he buried enough gold bars, which the Nazis had taken from banks all over Europe, to become a multimillionaire in today's world. Hillman used this newfound wealth to build himself a network of loyal followers. Corrupt officials in many countries were on his payroll. Hillman bragged that he had acquired a nuclear weapon from a corrupt Russian general who would sell any weapon for a price. It would seem that Hillman was willing to pay that price.

Hillman had developed an interesting view of history: his warped perceptions had convinced himself that history had not been changed at all. Instead, it was Alfred Hillman who was to lead the rebirth of Nazi supremacy in the world.

Mac and I did much more listening than talking when we were in Hillman's presence. We wanted to know as much about Hillman's plans as possible. One advantage I had was that Hillman didn't know I could speak and understand any language, including the one he had learned to speak in Brazil, Portuguese. Hillman had four or five men from Brazil in his employ. He spoke exclusively in Portuguese to these men. I tried to overhear as much as possible.

Mac asked Hillman what he wanted with us. Hillman told Mac that our job was to build one hundred Eradicator weapons. Mac then made what, at the time, seemed a tactical error in judgment. He told Hillman, "The Americans have the second Eradicator that had belonged to Krull, and without it, we couldn't build anymore of them." Hillman's eyes lit up when Mac said this. "I did not know that the Americans had the weapon. Let us see if they will give it to me in exchange for your lives."

Hillman gave me a telephone, turned on a device to scramble the call, and asked me to contact someone who had the authority to bring the remaining working Eradicator to him. I tried to tell Hillman that the Americans would never release this weapon to him under any circumstances. With a gun to my head, Hillman told me to make the phone call. I called Clem, and after a sentence or two of small talk, he asked me how I was doing. "Not great. Hillman is holding Mac and me hostage and he wants you to bring the Eradicator to him, or he is threatening to kill both of us." Clem said he couldn't do that.

At this point, Hillman hit the speakerphone button and spoke loudly, "I am not only holding these two men hostage, but I am also in possession of a fifty-megaton nuclear warhead. If you do not manufacture one hundred Eradicator weapons in perfect working order, I will detonate this nuclear bomb at a time and place of my choosing. If, however, you do supply me with these Hydro-Eradicator weapons, I will turn over the nuclear weapon to you and release the two scientists."

Clem said he needed time to look into the matter. Before Clem hung up, I mentioned that my lady was in London, and that Clem should tell her we were okay. He said that he would, then closed the conversation with, "Never a dull moment with you guys. Call me back in twenty-four hours." Even in this situation there was an element of humor in Clem's words that relaxed me. Our job now was to find out where Hillman had this nuclear weapon hidden. Mac was less optimistic about our immediate future, as he turned to me and whispered that he might be talking to the dead face-to-face pretty soon.

The lab Hillman had built was truly state of the art for the time. He had also spent much of his time over the past thirty years rounding up pieces of any and all meteorites known to have fallen to Earth. I asked Hillman if, in the event Mac and I were able to duplicate the Eradicators in large numbers, he would still turn the nuclear weapon over to the Americans. His "We'll see" answer was far less than assuring to me, though we had no intention of mass-producing these weapons for him under any circumstances.

So, as I had done during the war, I was once again working in Hillman's lab. We tried to look busy as we analyzed pieces of various meteorites looking for the rare unearthly element we called Tazniom. I actually found this element in the third chunk of rock sample I examined, in sufficient quantity to build at least thirty Eradicators. Of course, we had no intention of telling Hillman our findings. Mac and I were under guard, but the guards stood thirty feet from us in the lab. I thought they must have feared an explosion of some sort, so they kept their distance.

I told Mac our lives seemed to have a roller-coaster element to them. We would go through a five-year stretch that was fairly uneventful and even relaxing, then for a few months at a time we'd be at the center of a crisis. Mac did not disagree with me; he simply called it our fate in this timeline. We knew that we needed to find out quickly what Hillman had in mind. He had an office in the house next to a spare bedroom. I passed it a few times on the way to the bathroom. A few days after our capture, Hillman had an important meeting with two men in this office. I faked a fainting episode in the lab, and Mac told one of the guards I was in a diabetic shock and needed to lie down. Mac almost ordered these guards to take me to the bedroom next to Hillman's office.

One of the guards stood outside the front door as I put a stethoscope to the wall to try to overhear the conversation going on inside. Again, they spoke in Portuguese so they didn't feel the need to whisper. Earlier in that same day, I had complimented Hillman on his learning a new language and then told him that I had no such talent for languages. The only things I heard clearly were the words "missile" and "Beirut."

It made sense that the missile could be in Lebanon. Hillman hated Jews and the target could well be Israel. Add to that fact that Lebanon was run by Syria at that time; their leaders could be bribed without much difficulty. I had to figure out a way to get this information to Clem or Louise. I knew that if I could find a way, they in turn would tell Israeli intelligence.

My chance came the next day when Clem called back to tell Hillman that America needed proof that he had a nuclear weapon in his possession. I told Hillman in his anger at the question, to hand me the phone, which he surprisingly did.

"Trust me," I said, "he has this weapon. By the way, is my girlfriend there?" Clem said she was, so I assumed she was on another line listening in. I told Clem, "In case I never see her again, tell her that I had a great time on vacation in London, Tel Aviv, Beirut, Paris, and Florence."

Hillman grabbed the phone back, and sarcastically told me my words were "touching." "You want proof?" Hillman asked Clem in anger. "Pick up a Russian general named Yousenoff. He sold me the bomb for 10 million American dollars. I want those one hundred Eradicators in three days or I detonate the bomb." Hillman hung up.

Mac told Hillman he thought he gave up his Russian general friend pretty easily. Hillman called Yousenoff "An arrogant pig who didn't deserve the chance to spend my money." It was interesting that Hillman could see arrogance in others but never in himself. I realized something else about Hillman when he gave up his contact to acquire nuclear weapons: this could never be a long-term plan for the rise of the Fourth Reich. Hillman was going to attempt to kill as many Jews with one bomb as Hitler did during the entire war, no doubt to put himself in the history books next to his perverted idol.

In the three days Hillman waited for the American response to his absurd request, he had countless meetings and phone calls with third parties. In case his phone lines were bugged, Hillman would tell one of his lieutenants the message in person. The next step would be to send that man to another location to make the phone call to his agents in Beirut.

Mac and I underestimated Hillman's knowledge of the rare element Tazniom's being the key component to constructing Eradicator weapons. Hillman asked Mac if we had looked at the meteorite samples he had compiled for us to examine. Hillman strolled through the lab slowly and picked up the chunk of rock that I recognized as the #3 sample, which did indeed have Tazniom in it. Hillman asked Mac specifically if we had looked at this meteorite sample he was holding in his hand. Mac said that we had inspected it, and then Hillman simply said, "Well?" Mac said we didn't find any Tazniom in it. Hillman then took out his Luger from his pocket and shot Mac in the right thigh.

"If you lie to me again, the next bullet goes in your brain." Mac and I overlooked the fact that Hillman had Sigmund's handheld computer and was able to study it over the years to determine what made the Eradicators work, and Lord knows how many other facts he must have learned as well. We were certain that Hillman was using the unit to print money for himself, adding to his wealth. What Hillman could not figure out was the proper way to refine Tazniom to make it weapons-ready. Honestly, I knew vaguely of the tedious process required to refine it, but neither I nor Mac were certain of the step-by-step process. We were not weapons scientists, so we would only be guessing.

What I found more surprising was the fact that Hillman thought the Americans could make him one hundred Eradicators in three days. After all, they weren't able to duplicate one in almost forty years. Perhaps because the Americans had the remaining working unit, Hillman figured they could mass-produce them somehow. Anyway, I tied off Mac's gunshot wound as best I could to stop the bleeding, then got Mac on a table and I removed the bullet lodged in his leg. Fortunately, Hillman had a well-equipped lab, so getting the bullet out was less difficult than it could have been otherwise.

I told Mac after I took the bullet out that I really enjoyed putting that tongue depressor in his mouth to shut him up for awhile. Mac kept yelling, "It hurts, it hurts," before I took the bullet out. I never failed to remind him afterwards that he was a pussy when it came to pain. Hillman knew that I would be too busy trying to save Mac's life to try to escape. Who knows, maybe that was the real reason Hillman shot him.

Because it very well might save our lives, I began to try refining the meteorite's Tazniom, not to make weapons but to show Hillman we were making some progress and perhaps buy a little more time. After sixteen hours I realized I had no idea how to accomplish this refining process, and neither did Mac. Mac became Fred Sanford, lying on the table barking out orders while I, as Lamont, did all the real work. (Mac could really get on your nerves sometimes.) Hillman was awaiting Clem's call, and I hoped I would be within earshot, as Clem might be feeding me some kind of clue.

When the phone call did arrive, Hillman wanted me in the room, which was fortunate. Clem told Hillman that he would get his Eradicators as promised, if he turned over the nuke and told Clem where it was. Hillman turned down both requests. He insisted on receiving the Eradicators first. Clem refused. Clem then asked to speak with me to see if we were still alive. After Hillman handed me the phone and I said, "Hello". Clem said, "I wasn't going to give you a buffalo nickel for the chance you and Mac were still alive." From Clem's choice of words, I assumed the Eradicators were, indeed, being manufactured, but they would contain the non-working nickel in place of the chrome chip. That was the same sabotage I had accomplished on the alien ship many years ago.

Hillman took the phone and said these negotiations were less than useless, then hung up. As though a light switch went off in Hillman's head, in a split second he changed his plans. "It is time for me to attain my destiny in this world." Hillman now realized the Americans had no intention of turning over the Eradicators. Clem was making fake Eradicators to give Hillman, but it would make no difference. Hillman was determined to launch his nuclear weapon at Israel from Lebanon, and soon.

From this point forward, Mac and I were simply spectators to what unfolded. Hillman traveled to Lebanon, but before his plane had landed Mossad agents had located the missile base, thanks to American spy satellites. The Israeli agents also located the radioactive signature of the hydrogen bomb Hillman had purchased. After a brief firefight, the Mossad agents and Israeli Army SWAT teams that accompanied them got to the weapon and deactivated it. Hillman was kidnapped by the Israelis after his plane landed, and spent the rest of his life in an Israeli prison. This was a fitting end for Hillman, who was planning the destruction of the Jewish state. There was talk that Israel wanted to run a public trial of Hillman for war crimes, but Clem met with Israel's leaders privately to kill that idea, for obvious reasons.

Louise was part of a rescue team that came to Hillman's home and freed Mac and me. German police and a few American Special Forces people from Ramstein Air Force Base assisted in our rescue. Hillman's men had no stomach for a firefight. Knowing that my woman and my best friend from this timeline came to help save us made me tear up a bit. Mac and I were lucky men. One last point on that nuclear weapon: the Israelis said they destroyed it, but Clem was certain they boxed it up and sent it back to Israel. No matter, this latest crisis was over.

We took Mac back to his home in Switzerland to recuperate. Louise's sister offered to stay with Mac and nurse him back to health. Those two seemed to hit it off, and Louise and I just smiled when we left Mac's home to return to London to pick up Victoria. When we got back to London we stayed at Louise's flat for a few days, taking Victoria anywhere she wanted to go, from Piccadilly to Stonehenge. We read in the

London papers about the "Illegal Attack by Israel into Lebanon threatening to Destabilize the Country." This news headline really turned my stomach. The world press was so anti-Israel. I wondered to myself if this would be the case if Israel had oil fields too, but that discussion is best left for another day.

Clem went to Israel while Louise and I were in London, as he was making sure Hillman had a life sentence in solitary confinement with no press coverage. After Clem worked that out, he came to London so he could fly back with us to New York. On the flight to New York, Clem told me that he and his wife were getting a legal separation, stating irreconcilable differences. As Clem would often do to me, I hit him with a one-liner that made him smile: I told him that in my opinion he and his wife have had irreconcilable difference from the moment they met. Still, Clem obviously loved this woman, and was a bit somber when discussing it.

For most of the flight home, Victoria wanted every detail of what had happened in Germany. Of course, since the newspapers didn't know what had happened I couldn't tell Victoria much, though Clem seemed to enjoy my feeble attempts at dodging her questions. While Victoria took a nap, I asked Clem if he was really going to make Eradicators for Hillman. He assured me they indeed were almost finished. Clem admitted that the Americans tried to make copies many years ago, so they had many of the housings ready for assembly.

Louise spoke up in front of Clem to proclaim my brilliance in the coded message I had sent them over the telephone at Hillman's house. Clem agreed, saying that they were able to figure out that Tel Aviv was the target and Beirut was the launch point. The other three cities I mentioned on the phone were actual places we vacationed in, so they were eliminated from consideration. Clem then called the Mossad and ordered U.S. intelligence satellites to focus in on southern Lebanon.

All I said on the matter was that the three of us made a great team. When we got back to my apartment, I felt ready to sleep for a week. We actually lived a normal life for a time after that. The highlight of our new talent for languages was that Louise and I were finally able to communicate with our Polish cleaning woman.

The years passed, and as we aged into our sixties we were dealing with much more mundane problems. My proctologist, after sticking his gloved finger up my rear end so far that I thought he would have hit China, informed me that he didn't like the increased size of my prostate gland. The biopsy he performed next was negative for cancer, but he wanted to see me every six months, so he could "stay intimate" with me. I must say that of all the doctors I've met, proctologists have the best sense of humor.

CHAPTER 35

THE LOSS OF LOUISE

Louise became a bit distant a few months later, and I couldn't put my finger on why. She was so closed-mouthed about things that I could rarely get a good read on her. One evening, when Victoria was at a sleepover with a friend, Louise told me, quite casually, that she had breast cancer. I never felt so helpless. Louise neglected treatment for too long, and the cancer had spread. I tried giving the sphere to Louise to hold, as I prayed this would work to cure her, but it did not. Louise would be dead within three months.

Before Louise died she told me I might be Victoria's father; it was either me or an MI-6 agent she worked with. I told Louise it didn't matter who the actual father was, and I would take care of Victoria as my own. I was devastated that there was nothing else I could do. I asked Clem to contact the Rell to see if they could help us, but they could or would not. We told Victoria of her mother's illness and she handled it well on the outside, but what she went through in the privacy of her own room was not hard to imagine.

Louise's sister offered to have Victoria live with her and Mac in Switzerland. After the funeral I gave the choice to Victoria, but she preferred to stay with me. I am not elaborating on the three-month-long fight Louise had at the end of her life, as it is too painful for me to think about again. Louise fought until her last breath. I wish I possessed half her strength of will. She should have died in battle, not from a silent killer like breast cancer.

After Louise died, Clem asked if he could move in with me for awhile. Clem's wife kept the house in the separation, and since he was a rare government official who was not on someone's payroll, Clem didn't have the money to get an apartment of his own. It was a good deal for both of us.

CHAPTER 36
MY NEW ROOMMATE

We took my king-size bed out of the master bedroom and put in two queen-sized ones. Victoria called us the "Odd Couple," which we honestly were. In case anyone reading this is wondering, I was the neat one. Victoria was nineteen years old at this point, and she had a mysterious boyfriend I wanted to meet. She kept telling me I'd meet him before they moved in together. That was less than reassuring to me. Clem was egging me on to find out for certain if I was the biological father. Without my knowledge, he took some of Victoria's hair from a brush in the bathroom, and sent it to his buddies in the lab at Groom Lake.

Before Clem got the results from the brush, he told me that he had retired. As he put it, the young guns "pushed him out," saying, "Sixty-three's a little old for this line of work." Clem was a little bitter at how the end of his "official" working life came to be; however, he understood it. The most important job that I had to learn now was to be able to shoot rubber bands with force and accuracy. Victoria worked with me diligently to improve the speed of the rubber band shot, and to hit my target. When Victoria asked me why I wanted to learn to do this, I told her it was because Clem snored.

Victoria laughed so hard she starting choking, but I was dead serious. A few nights later, when I was a good enough shot to hit what I was aiming at, I took twenty rubber bands into bed with me. Whenever Clem was sleeping flat on his back, he snored so loud the oxygen seemed to be sucked out of the room. I would take a rubber band and shoot Clem in the stomach, and this would cause him to roll over on his side, giving me fifteen minutes of silence before the process started again. The next morning, Clem said, "There was a damn mosquito biting me all night." Then he saw the twenty rubber bands in bed with him, and we both started laughing.

Clem received a Federal Express the next day. When he opened the envelope, I saw a sad look come over him. He asked me to sit down. Clem knew I was beginning to think I really was Victoria's biological father, because we recently had discovered that we had the same blood type. Clem looked at his feet as he spoke to me, and then put it to me this way: "I took some hair from Victoria's brush and sent it to Nevada for testing. I know I shouldn't have done it, that it was none of my business. But I did do it, and now I have the answer in my hands. Do you want to know if you're the biological father or not?"

The way Clem phrased that, he put me in a corner. When I told him to tell me, he kept teasing me with lines like, "I'll burn this note now and never mention it again." I almost wrung his neck as he began laughing and told me to put a curfew on that daughter of mine. I grabbed that piece of paper out of his hand so fast the naked eye might have missed it. Victoria was indeed my daughter in every way.

Victoria got home from NYU, where she was currently a sophomore. After spending hours trying to get my confidence up, I finally told Victoria that I was her biological father. All she said was, "Yeah, I know, Mom told me." I felt like an idiot. Victoria went on to tell me that her mother didn't want me to know for certain that I was the biological father, because in that way I wouldn't feel obligated to bring Victoria up if I didn't want to. It would be my choice. Clem and I were surprised, but Louise's logic made sense.

As her father, I thought it was time to meet the boyfriend. He was named Mickey and he was twenty-five years old, which was scary to me, as that was six years older than Victoria. Mickey had a two-man business selling reptiles to local New York and New Jersey pet stores. After graduation from college, Mickey traveled to Southeast Asia, South America, and Africa to make connections to get his exotic pets. He certainly sounded like a resourceful young man. Clem wanted to meet him too.

Victoria was so much like her mother, it was amazing. She was low-key about almost everything. Victoria had no objection to inviting Mick, as she called him, to dinner for cross-examination. Clem and I were looking to find fault in this young man, as we both felt that there was too much of an age difference between a boy of twenty-five and girl of nineteen. However, we were both taken by him. He immediately reminded me of my partner in my old telescope business: young and good looking, with endless energy and a bubbly personality. After meeting him, Clem and I both wanted to adopt him. Mickey was also the funniest storyteller I have ever met. He told us stories of his escapades in the reptile business.

Mick's parents were both dead and I sensed that he was beginning to attach himself to us, as he knew we really liked him. Defender even seemed to take to Mick, which was unusual since he didn't like most strangers. Clem still did double-takes every time he looked at Defender, because of the incredible resemblance to our alien friend. After dinner, we three men all sat down in the living room. Victoria excused herself to give the boys "some room." I asked Mickey how he got started in this unusual business. Listening to him for the next hour, Clem and I never laughed so hard in our lives.

Mickey said that he and his partner Ed grew up together and both loved lizards, turtles, and snakes. They came up with a business plan to spend each of their grandfathers' inheritance monies (as both boys had them) to start a reptile wholesaling business. Mickey flew around the world trying to make business connections while Ed went around to local pet shops asking which reptiles they wished to have in the store, but had trouble getting. Mickey went on to say that they started keeping all the animals in his grandmother's basement. When I asked Mickey if his grandmother knew she had snakes in her basement, he simply said, "I looked her right in the eye and swore that we had no snakes down there." Mickey was the smoothest liar I had ever encountered. I honestly think that he could beat any lie detector test ever invented.

Clem was fascinated with this business of Mickey's, as well. Clem chimed in, "Did your grandmother ever find out?"

"Well, one day I was back in Boston visiting an old girlfriend when Ed got a call from my grandmother. It seemed she was having lunch at the kitchen table and a big black snake had joined her, coiled up just a foot or two away. Ed handled things very calmly. He went over and grabbed the black indigo snake that had escaped and put him back in his cage downstairs. Ed told me that my grandmother said to him, 'You know, Mickey promised me that there were no snakes in my basement.' Ed said, 'Mrs. Melman, we both know that Mickey often has trouble telling the truth. He probably didn't want to scare you.'"

Mickey had a way of putting himself down in these stories of his that was just too funny for words. He went on to say that before his grandmother threw them out of her home, a four-foot monitor lizard escaped, bit through Mrs. Melman's washing machine hose, and escaped through a basement window. Two days later, the neighbor's cat was missing.

They also lost a tarantula in his grandmoth/ was never found. I know that's not funny, but whⅇⅈ told the story you had to laugh. Mickey went on to say that his grandmother threw them out, obviously with excellent reasons, so Mickey and Ed got a store. Almost immediately, the neighboring stores got a petition together to get them thrown out. The Persian rug dealer next door was the leader of the anti-reptile movement, demanding that the landlord throw them out or he and six other tenants on the block would break their leases and move elsewhere.

The landlord gave in to the pressure and sent Mickey an eviction notice, and as he told us this story, he got very angry. "I told Ed, we are Americans in America, and this Iranian piece of shit starts a petition to throw us out? He will pay for this." Clem and I were rolling with laughter, waiting to hear how Mickey got even with the petition-wielding Persian. "We had 10,000 crickets from Flucker's Cricket farm in Louisiana. The crickets were used as food for the lizards. I drilled a hole from our store into the Persian rug store and used a paper towel roll to connect the cricket box through the wall into the asshole's rug store. We released 10,000 crickets into his store the night before we were evicted. Those large rolls of carpet were a perfect hiding place for the crickets. Yeah, we heard it took him six months to find them all."

Clem and I were roaring, and we wanted more stories. Victoria stuck her nose out to see us laughing, smiled, and went back to her room. Mickey then told of us his parrot Paco, a yellow nape. He said when he lived at home before his mom died, Paco would listen every night as Mickey's mom would yell, "Mickey, time for dinner." Mickey said his mom had an ear-piercing voice, and even now, ten years after his mom passed away, he still has to listen to her voice through the bird calling him to dinner day and night, in a perfect imitation. When Mickey told us he felt that his mother was cursing him from the grave, Clem and I almost rolled off of our chairs in laughter. You had to love this kid.

Mickey took a break at this point and asked us what we did when we were younger. Clem said he worked for the government. Mickey said, "Hiding in a government cubicle, waiting for your thirty years to go by so you could collect the pension?"

Clem smiled, "Yeah, something like that."

Then Mickey asked me what I did. I told him I was a scientist, to which Mickey replied, "I'll bet the pay sucks, huh?"

Victoria came out to join the conversation. "Glad to see you are all having such a good time together." Mickey excused himself to go to the bathroom, and then Clem and I both told her to hang onto this kid; if his business ever were to fail, he could easily make a living as a stand-up comedian. Victoria agreed, telling us that she knew he was a bit of a bullshit artist, but he had so much positive energy, he was fun to be around. The doorbell rang at this point and Defender started barking so loudly that Clem had a hand on his gun, as he was figuring the dog maybe knew something. There were two Mossad agents at our door. Mickey came out of the bathroom to see these two men being shown into our living room.

For the first time all night, Mickey was speechless. The Mossad agents asked to speak to us in private, so Mickey and Victoria went to her room. They asked a lot of questions about Hillman, who he was, where he came from. The Israelis weren't stupid, but Clem made them feel that way. Clem told these men he went over all this with their superiors back in Israel. Clem was yelling so loudly half the building must have heard him. Clem refused to give these Israeli agents the information they desired, but instead made a promise to the Mossad that the United States intelligence services would "owe them one" if they kept Hillman in solitary confinement for the rest of his life and not ask any questions.

The Mossad agents were clearly frustrated by not getting the answers they had hoped for, but they took Clem's IOU quite seriously, and said he would be hearing from Israeli intelligence shortly. There obviously was something the Israelis had in mind to collect on this IOU. I understood their frustration. The Mossad had in their custody a Nazi who claimed to be from the twenty-second century, who had come back in time, somehow, got into Hitler's inner circle, buried millions in gold, and almost annihilated Israel with a fifty-megaton nuclear warhead perched in Lebanon.

All things considered, I was very surprised they left without the answers they sought, but then again, Clem was a powerful man in the U.S. intelligence field, retired or not. An IOU from Clem was worth quite a bit to Israel. Mickey and Victoria came out of Victoria's room like they were shot out of a cannon. Mickey asked Clem, "I guess you weren't the 'hide-in-your-cubicle-and-wait-for-retirement type' after all." Victoria talked Clem and me and her mother up for several hours that evening. She told Mickey all the stories we had told her and Mickey was more than fascinated. Mickey told us later that evening that he wanted to be a spy now, too.

We asked Mickey "why?" He had an interesting job and was making decent money. Mickey put his head down a bit, and admitted that the United States government had recently put him out of business. Mickey's last story of the night was that a shipment of supposed reticulated pythons from Thailand came into Lufthansa cargo at Kennedy airport. Mickey swore to us that this was the truth, that he did not order any poisonous snakes, but when the Fish and Wildlife people opened the crate, there were only pit vipers inside. The government fined him $14,000 per snake, which effectively put Mickey and his partner out of business. Mickey couldn't believe he had lost the case; the manifest had listed only reticulated pythons.

Mickey gave us the final chapter in his short-lived career selling reptiles. As he put it, aside from having tortoise races within giant circles, putting numbers on the turtle's backs and taking bets on them, he was unemployed. Mickey then asked if he could bring his closest friend over to meet us. Freddy Weiner was a professional escape artist who was between jobs but would make a great spy too, as Mickey put it. Clem told Mickey to calm down with all the spy talk. Mickey seemed disappointed after Clem told him to calm down, so Clem threw him a bone and asked Mickey to invite his friend over. "What is his stage name?" I asked.

"The Great Weenie," Mickey said.

With that, Clem laughed, "No wonder he's unemployed."

A few days later, Mickey and his friend with the ridiculous stage name were coming over after dinner. Clem was perplexed because he wanted to help Mickey and his friend, but you don't just snap your fingers and make someone a spy. Years of training were involved in this line of work. I sensed Clem's frustration, and told him to just be straight with the kids and tell them what it would take. Clem agreed. I had a similar problem with Victoria, as she wanted to drop out of school and become a spy too, following in her mom's footsteps.

As a quick aside, there was a second reason Mickey was coming over: we had been getting more of a cockroach problem of late, particularly in the area of the kitchen sink. Mickey swore to me that he could solve this problem we were having without any pesticides. I was looking forward to finding out his solution to this pesky problem. At eight o'clock that evening Mickey arrived with his friend Freddy Weiner.

CHAPTER 37

THE GREAT WEENIE

Freddy was very slight of build, perhaps 5 feet 5 inches tall, weighing no more than 145 pounds. He was meek at first, but opened up as the night wore on. Mickey had a Chinese-food takeout box with him which I thought held food, but the box contained three lion-tailed flying geckoes. Mickey said these lizards were able to eat cockroaches because of their great night vision. The geckoes had suction-cupped feet, which meant they could climb any surface. Mickey assured us this would solve our problem; Clem and I were more than a bit skeptical. Mickey said the geckoes were afraid of humans, so they would never bother us. Having these prehistoric-looking reptiles climbing our walls at night would give me a second reason for not sleeping, or as Victoria put it, "You're up anyway, so give it a chance." Victoria loved this gecko plan, so I went along with it.

What Mickey neglected to mention regarding these geckoes was the noises they made after they caught their prey, somewhere between a bullfrog croak and a human groan. Trying to sleep that night between Clem's snoring and the groans of the geckoes having their midnight snack was almost driving me insane.

Anyway, back to the after-dinner conversation and performance. Mickey told Freddy to bring all his toys with him to our apartment that evening. In the next two hours, we saw "The Great Weenie" get out of handcuffs and a straightjacket, several incredible sleight-of-hand tricks, and his invisibility trick, where he threw a sheet over himself and then seemed to disappear.

Clem was very impressed with the bizarre talents of "The Great Weenie," and I saw the wheels turning in his head. Clem took Freddy's address and phone number, and talked to both young men about the rigorous training required to become a field operative with one of the major agencies. The boys were not deterred at all, and Clem was taking them seriously into his heart with plans for both young men.

Several days later I called Clem's wife on the phone, told her how much Clem missed her and wanted to get back together with her. She softened quite a bit after that, and said she'd consider it. Days later, she called me back and agreed to meet and talk with Clem. Clem knew nothing of this plan, which I was doing to get his snoring ass out of my bedroom. When Clem got home later, I simply told him that his wife called and wanted to talk about getting back together. Clem pulled up his pants with confidence and told me that he knew it was only a matter of time until she came around. I just smiled.

Several weeks later I got a phone call from Pam, Louise's sister, in Switzerland. Mac had had a stroke, leaving the left side of his body nearly useless. Pam also told me that Mac said after this stroke happened, he lost his ability to hear the thoughts of the dead. On my flight over to see Mac I was thinking that I was the only one left with a gift from the Defender. Louise was dead, and Mac had lost his ability. Only my skill for languages remained. I had passing thoughts of anger toward the Defender for not intervening somehow to save Louise from her cancer and Mac from his debilitating stroke, but part of me knew that life had to play out naturally, except under the most extreme circumstances.

It broke my heart to see Mac in that wheelchair, with his left arm limp and his left leg just dead weight. He spoke as if he had marbles in his mouth, making him very difficult to understand. I stayed with Mac for a week, and as each day passed, the look in his eyes grew dimmer. He wanted to die, not live like this; that's what his eyes were telling me.

Pam was an angel, staying with Mac right to the end. I prayed for the Defender, if indeed he was still watching over us, to take Mac as soon as possible. Mac died the same day as Thurman Munson in the summer of 1979. I told Clem I wanted to go to Yankee Stadium for that game against the Baltimore Orioles, after Thurman's and Mac's death. It was cathartic. Fifty-five thousand people were crying as the Yankees took the field that night, when no catcher came out to home plate. Lou Piniella, Bobby Murcer, Reggie Jackson, the whole team, the whole crowd at the game, and millions watching at home were in tears. This was what my timeline did not have: we didn't have soul. The Nazis had taken that from the people of my timeline. What we were able to accomplish in changing history, was to allow this moment of sorrow to happen. Mourning a death together can nourish the soul.

Pam told us Mac wanted to be cremated, and his ashes brought back to the basement in Berlin where we materialized in 1938. I had no objection. Pam was first going to bring the ashes to New York, and stay with us. Thankfully, Clem was back with his wife, so Pam could stay with us for as long as she liked. After a death such as this, we all wanted the comfort of people who knew that person well, to tell stories and share the mutual sadness we all felt.

Clem had called in a few favors, and got both Mickey and his friend Freddy into an offshoot department of the CIA. Some people called this service Black Ops. It was most unusual to be brought straight from the street into this program, but Clem was still an incredibly powerful influence in these circles. I was beginning to think that Clem did not really retire at all, as he seemed to still have his hand in many things.

Years passed, and Victoria graduated from college and wanted to join a clandestine intelligence service of some kind. She was still in a relationship with Mickey when time permitted, but their passion for each other had cooled because of distance. I knew in my heart that Victoria would make a great spy like her mother, but to recommend and condone this life was tough for a father to do. When your daughter says things to you like, "As an attractive woman I can use my body to get information from male agents or suspects, which is such an advantage for me because no male agent could do it," how is a father supposed to react positively to a statement like that? She was right, of course, but I couldn't very well tell her that. Yet I saw so much of her mother in her that in the end, I could not stand in her way. Clem made a phone call, and Victoria was on her way to CIA headquarters in Langley, Virginia, for training.

CHAPTER 38

THE BREAKOUT

A few weeks later the Israelis showed up one night to talk to Clem, who was no longer living with me, but happened to be over for cigars and brandy. The Mossad was calling in their IOU. An Israeli spy had been apprehended near Moscow, and he had hidden a list of the names of seventeen other Israeli agents working inside the Soviet Union. The Mossad wanted Clem's help to try to break him out, negotiate his release, or, as a last resort, kill him so he couldn't talk.

Clem told the agents he would see what he could do. Clem contacted the man heading the training of Mickey and Freddy, and asked how ready they were to do some overseas work. Clem was pleased to hear that they were fast learners, and quite capable of such a mission. Three nights later, Mickey and Freddy came to my apartment for a briefing. Clem had his faults, but he sure was a great general in the intelligence field. He had a knack for seeing many moves ahead in these dangerous situations.

It was late April 1986 when Clem met with Mickey and Freddy to devise a plan to get the Israeli agent out of a Moscow prison. I tried to talk Clem out of the idea of using two such "green" agents in this most dangerous of missions. Clem just kept saying, "Calm down and trust me." The Russians were preoccupied with the nuclear disaster at Chernobyl. Clem told me that when the nuclear reactor exploded, the blast and subsequent radiation was 400 times greater than the

A-bomb America dropped on Hiroshima. Belarus was hardest hit by the fallout from this radioactive cloud. The Russians would be cleaning this up for ten years, and it would cost billions.

Back to the plan: using fake Canadian passports, Mickey and Freddy were traveling to Moscow as vodka importers. Freddy and Mickey had miniature homing devices implanted in the heels of their shoes. The plan was for Mickey to tell the Russian police that Freddy was an American spy, so he would get thrown into the same prison as the Israeli agent. Then, using his skills to escape, Freddy would free himself, find the Israeli and free him as well. A diversion would be created on the other side of the prison so they could make their escape to the American Embassy. A car would be waiting. This is simplistic, but the basic plan.

Freddy would have a wire which he used as a lock pick with him, hidden in a false-skin pouch surgically put in his left forearm. He would use this wire to escape his handcuffs and then jail cell. Something about the plan seemed fishy to me, but I couldn't put my finger on it, so I said nothing at the time. The morning after Mickey had left for Moscow, Victoria "had to tell me" that she made passionate love to Mickey the night before, to give him the confidence to carry out his mission. Sometimes I think Victoria just wanted to torture me.

The plan at first seemed to work as it was drawn up. Freddy was placed in a cell two doors down from the Israeli spy. After waiting until 3 a.m., Freddy escaped from his prison cell and knocked on the Israeli's door. Freddy had some difficulty, but he finally managed to open the door to the Mossad agent's cell. At the prescribed time, there was indeed a diversion created on the other side of the prison compound. The last step in the plan failed, as the prison guard that was supposedly paid off to leave the outside gate open, failed to do so, and they were recaptured.

The Israeli agent was beaten severely, and told the Russian secret police where the list with the agent's names was hidden. Freddy was beaten as well, but not half as badly. Mickey had been sitting in the car outside the prison, and when he saw the Russian military police approaching his car he took off in his vehicle. It took the Russians two hours to capture him as he led them on a chase for the ages, but in the end he was finally apprehended. Mickey was sent to the same prison as Freddy and the Israeli agent. This time, they were all in the same cell with two guards watching them.

Clem got a phone call from the Mossad informing him of the situation. I had no idea at that time what was going on. Clem casually asked me if I still had that metal ball the Defender gave me. I nodded yes, and then Clem made a phone call. The next thing I knew, we were flying to Moscow. I asked what we were doing, and Clem said, "We're picking up the kids." We were met at the airport by the number three man in the Russian power hierarchy. We were driven directly to his home.

For most of the one-hour ride to his home outside Moscow, this man was sitting in the back seat with us, coughing and hacking away. I thought he had the flu, but it turned out that his thyroid gland was radioactive. The party official had been in Belarus when the reactor at Chernobyl exploded; he had developed radiation sickness and would probably be dead in a month. Unbeknownst to me, Clem had made a deal with this high-ranking Russian official. Clem would save his life in exchange for the release of the three prisoners.

The exchange worked this way: the Russian Politburo official called the prison from his home to have Mickey, Freddy and Avram (the Israeli agent) released and then driven to the American embassy; from there a chartered plane would fly the three of them to Helsinki, Finland. Once they landed in Finland, Clem and I would give the Russian the cure to his radiation sickness. We would be held captive if we failed to save his life.

Clem didn't want the Russians to know anything about the sphere, so he made up a story about an experimental drug that I was going to administer by injection. The injection I gave this man was simply to put him to sleep. Clem coyly slipped the metallic ball into his hand after he fell asleep, and then told the guards that he should sleep for an hour and then he'd be fine. I realized at that moment that I had been surrounded by the best liars in the world. From Louise and Clem to my daughter and Mickey too, they were all so good at look-you-in-the-eye deception.

Outside the Politburo member's bedroom, I chatted with his personal bodyguards and doctors, in Russian. They were impressed with my language skills. My main goal was to befriend them as best I could, just in case the sphere had lost its touch. An hour later we walked back into the room, and Clem then palmed the sphere from the Russian's hand to his own, as the formerly radioactive Russian began to awaken. The doctors pushed us aside and started doing tests. The thyroid gland was no longer radioactive. We had to stay for two days until all the test results were returned. Igor, the Politburo member whom we had saved, was feeling so happy that he showed us around his home in great detail. He was strangely proud of the fact that he had stolen half of his art works from around the globe. It was understandable that he was so happy: we had just saved his life. He was cured, he thanked us, and we dodged his doctor's questions about this experimental drug and then flew to Helsinki.

On the flight to Helsinki, I was angry that a man like that had his obnoxious life saved while Louise and Mac had to die. It was a passing anger that rolled through my mind. When we got to the American embassy in Helsinki, I found out some more intriguing news. The Israelis were on their way to arrest the spy who had been imprisoned with Mickey and Freddy. Apparently, Israel was furious that he had given up the names of other spies to the Russians.

Mickey and Freddy had shocked looks on their faces when their new friend Avram was taken away in handcuffs through the back door of the American embassy. Clem was stone-faced and showed no emotion at all. We all boarded a chartered flight back to Washington for a debriefing. On the plane, Freddy said that he no longer wanted to be a spy, that this experience had left a sour taste in his mouth. Mickey wanted to stay in the spy game, but was looking forward to more domestic, less life-threatening work for a while.

Clem said nothing as Mickey and Freddy vehemently complained about the way the Israelis were treating Avram, by taking him away in handcuffs after he was beaten within an inch of his life. I knew Clem was playing his cards close to his vest, so I just tried to console the boys as best I could. I complimented them on a job well done. They both had done everything expected of them.

At the debriefing, Clem was chastised by the Defense Secretary for a reckless plan that had not been approved by him. Clem apologized and ate some humble pie, the boys told their story as they knew it, and then the final question came to Clem. "How did you manage to get these men released from a Soviet prison and flown to Helsinki?" Clem looked at the Defense Secretary and said, "A certain member of the Politburo owed me a favor." The Defense Secretary was fuming he was forced to settle for this vague answer. Mickey and Freddy were kept a few more days in Washington, filling out reports and such. Clem and I returned to New York.

The next evening Clem came over to escape his wife's latest rant, and as we sat down for cigars and brandy, which was becoming a regular event, I asked Clem to tell me what the true story was. After several brandies and a few "what do you mean?" comments, Clem finally came clean and told me the whole story.

First off, Clem said the boys were supposed to be recaptured after their daring escape. In this way, the Russians would believe that the list the Israeli agent was carrying was indeed genuine. The thinking was that if you risk other agents to save one, he must have important and truthful information. The Israeli prisoner did not talk before the boys attempted the rescue, but he was now free to give the list of false names to the Russians. The names he gave up were actually of Russian double agents and arms dealers, most of whom would sell their sister for a price.

I was fascinated by the complexity and simplicity of this plan. Clem also knew that the Russian Politburo member who was dying of radiation sickness would do anything to save his own life. Clem had this whole plan down from the beginning. Once I told him I thought the sphere was still working, everything else fell into place. Even the taking away of the Israeli spy, in handcuffs, was staged for the Russian agents across the street from the American embassy in Helsinki, who had been watching from their car.

Clem said the hardest part of the plan was not being able to tell Mickey and Freddy the truth, or the Defense Secretary either. Clem didn't want any leaks. Clem laughingly told me that he had the Defense Secretary's office bugged so maybe the Russians did, too. Clem then paid me an unexpected compliment. He said that I was the only person he'd tell the complete truth to, so that must make me his best friend. Clem was 100 percent correct in his logic; telling no one else the complete plan was the correct course of action. Of course, having the Defense Secretary furious with you, and Mickey and Freddy disappointed in you, was a steep price to pay to protect the covert actions of this plan. As Clem later said, "Now my debt to the Israelis is paid in full."

CHAPTER 39

DECODING THE DISTANT PAST

Louise's sister Pam returned to England to live out her years, which left me alone in my apartment for the first time in a long while. Alone except, of course, for my faithful dog Defender, and the three geckoes that belched all night long after feeding on a dinner of kitchen sink roaches. I had a neighbor's son come in and walk Defender for me, which made keeping him a lot easier. I passed my time reading dead languages and sending transcriptions to the various universities that had sent them over to me for evaluation. I felt useful in this way. My favorite readings were the oldest writings on Earth, ancient cuneiform from as far back as 3200 BC. The Defender had truly given me an incredible gift that allowed me to understand these writings.

Clem stopped over and saw what I was doing with the ancient cuneiform translations, and he smiled and said, "Come with me, I've got something much older for you to decode. Jeff, I'm gonna blow your mind, and then you're going to blow mine! Pack a bag." The next thing I knew, we were on a plane for North Dakota to a secret base in the Black Hills. Clem seemed embarrassed that he had forgotten to tell me about the discovery in North Dakota before this. He apologized for having been so preoccupied with getting the kids safely out of Moscow.

I told Clem I really hoped this wasn't more dead cattle or other animals that needed examining. He assured me it was nothing like that at all. With that said, we were driven to a base where I was to examine twenty-three large pieces of rock that were locked away in an underground ravine. My first reaction was that I wasn't a geologist, and why was I here? But Clem assured me that this would be an incredible day of discovery for everyone.

I was introduced to several members of the military clergy who, obviously, had clearance to be here. I now wondered aloud what was going on, and why men of the cloth were here at all. It didn't take long to find out. There were twenty-three large chunks of stone that had been recently discovered after dynamiting out a cavern several thousand feet deep. I surmised that the military was excavating to create either a nuclear silo or perhaps to do an underground nuclear test, but whatever the reason, the stones had been uncovered.

Each stone, by an inscribing method as yet unclear, contained writings of unknown origin. The inscriptions looked as though someone used a laser engraving tool to somehow burn the words into the rock face. The writings were 155 million years old. Cuneiform, which was the oldest known written language on Earth, was perhaps only 5,200 years old. This discovery was huge. No wonder the clergy were here. Perhaps they figured that these were ancient versions of the Ten Commandments, or something like that. A military rabbi, constantly davening, seemed to be next to me wherever I went. He was quite annoying. I became very uncomfortable around all these religious men, as I tried to work on piecing these stones together to be able to read them in any kind of order. The whole scene was totally bizarre. A bulldozer was used to pick up one chunk of rock and move it to where I directed.

This was a jigsaw puzzle played with fifty-ton boulders. Thanks to the gift the Defender had given me, I was able to read this unknown, never-before-seen-on-Earth language. It took over a week to line up the rocks correctly, and there were a few chunks of rock still missing from this puzzle, but I was able to get the drift of what it said. The first four stones spoke of where the aliens came from, a place they referred to as the TAL Galaxy.

As I continued to read the stones, I was suspended in mid-air by wires and a harness, trying to use my tape recorder without getting motion sickness. I was seemingly floating in air like Peter Pan. The writing within these stones was so large that you truly needed an aerial view to read them properly. As I tried to continue translating the alien writing into English, the clergymen who were hoping for a message from God in these inscriptions kept interrupting me with questions. I learned early on to just ignore them and do my work. What I had found out after reading all of the stones was quite different from what the religious men were hoping for.

It turns out that alien races came to Earth to wager on the outcomes of battles between various dinosaurs! Apparently, 155 million years ago, the planet Earth was to distant alien races what Las Vegas is to present-day humans. Our planet was a gambling haven for several alien species. The words that were, quite literally, written in stone were the outcomes of various matches recorded in a way that would survive time. Before I let anyone else know what I had just found out, I called Clem. Clem had left for Nevada on business but returned shortly after I called him.

When I told Clem my findings, he just shook his head in amazement. "So, like we bet on boxing matches or cock-fights, these aliens bet on who would win a fight between different species of dinosaurs. Unbelievable." To be technically correct, I told Clem that sometimes the fights were staged between the same species of dinosaur, too. It also was clear that these matches were recorded on something similar to television and, no doubt, sent back to their home planets as entertainment. When I asked Clem what I should tell the round-collar types walking about, he said, "Tell 'em the truth. I'm sure they'll bury the story for us. I don't think these guys want to tell the world that Earth was a gambling hall for alien races."

Clem was right again. I had to explain my findings to about twenty people in a conference room. At first they all thought that I was kidding, but then as they came to realize that I was being completely honest with them, disappointment became evident on their faces. The military types laughed, and the clergy stormed out of the room unsatisfied. I also told them that the aliens used some sort of a laser carving tool from orbit to inscribe these rocks with the results of individual battles. This indicated to me that perhaps the aliens on board their ships in orbit were able to keep track of the wins and losses of the dinosaur fights on Earth and transmit this information back to their home worlds. It seemed North Dakota was one of their favorite venues for these battles.

The priests and rabbi were suspicious of my findings. They correctly stated that since I was the only person on Earth who could "supposedly" read these writings, how were they to know that I had told them the truth? I could have been an atheist or devil worshipper who didn't want the word of God released to the masses. I walked away and let Clem defend my findings. Frankly, I was tired, cranky, and in need of a shower. I clearly wasn't in the mood to get into a religious argument.

I returned to New York a few days later. The whole dinosaur story had been disavowed, and all findings were classified. Honestly, I didn't know what the big deal was. So what if ancient alien races came to Earth to wager on dinosaur fights? How would this information alter anything in the everyday lives of people living today?

Freddy and Mickey came over to see me a few days later, even though Victoria wasn't living with me anymore. She was now stationed at the American Embassy in London. Freddy was about to return to the stage using the stage name "Freddy the Great" which was, in my opinion, a distinct improvement from "The Great Weenie." We were all having an excellent discussion about life when there came a knock on the door, which had to go under the category of "what can happen next?"

CHAPTER 40

BUSTED

Two Secret Service agents came to arrest me for counterfeiting. My first reaction was to laugh. I just wish it hadn't happened in front of the young men I had grown to like, whose respect I had gained. The comical aspect was that I had been using my handheld computer to make various currencies for fifty years, and it took the Secret Service that long to catch me. Mickey and Freddy tried desperately to vouch for my character, saying this had to be a mistake. However, I reassured the boys that I would handle this, and they should both let their blood pressure levels return to normal.

I realized something else as I was walked out of my apartment in handcuffs. If Clem were not still alive, I might not have been able to talk my way out of this arrest at all. No one else alive had the knowledge of what had transpired in my life, and I had no proof Clem had given me permission to use my computer to make money. Clem was back in Nevada and wasn't answering his cell phone, so I spent two days in jail. I met some very interesting characters in this federal jail cell. One man claimed that he was a graphic artist and just out of curiosity, he meticulously copied a $100 bill, on both sides, just to see how close he could come to a perfect duplicate. The man convinced me, but I found out later that he had been arrested seventeen times in fourteen different countries for attempting to make plates of various currencies.

The other man I met was a deserter from the army. He was a quiet young man who said he had made a mistake joining the military in the first place. His main complaint about the army was that he didn't like having to wake up so early. You had to chuckle at that. Clem finally arrived, apologetic that he had been incommunicado for so long. I told him it wasn't too bad, and I was released.

Clem also got a kick out of the fact that it took these guys so long to find me. "You've been making these bills with the same serial number for fifty years. It's good to know my tax dollars are hard at work." The sarcasm was dripping off of him. I asked Clem to put something in writing, somewhere, to pardon me if this were ever to happen again. He agreed. I was strangely famous for a week or two, because the *New York Post* headlines read "75-Year Old Counterfeiter Arrested on Upper West Side." Since most of my life was shrouded in secrecy, it was enjoyable to be able to talk to my neighbors about something. I would have preferred something legal, but things could have been worse. Clem called the *Post* and demanded that they print a retraction or at least note that I had been released. There was a small type-face box in the lower left corner of page 22, saying "75-Year Old Counterfeiter Released from Custody."

The whole incident bothered Clem much more than it did me. I called Mickey and Freddy to explain that my arrest had been a mistake. I didn't want them to think less of me because I had been led away in handcuffs. I wondered how the newspaper knew that I was seventy-five years old, but then I realized that some of the false documents I carried showed a corresponding birth date.

I went to the opening of Freddy's new off-off-Broadway show. It was a very small venue which seated only twenty people, but it seemed Freddy was thrilled to be out of the spy game. It was a shame that we were never able to tell Mickey and Freddie the truth. Maybe if they knew that they had actually been successful in their mission, Freddy might have stayed in the CIA.

After eating a late-night snack at home, with only my memories and loyal dog Defender at my side for company, I thought to myself that Victoria's being in London with her aunt Pam was a good thing for both of them. My thoughts drifted to Louise, and how proud she would have been of Victoria's following in her footsteps.

That same night I had the strangest dream, which may not have been a dream at all. Mac came to me in my sleep and said that he had gotten a job in the Soul Services deployment division. I heard Mac telling a Rell employee that Louise's soul would be returned to Earth in short order, due to the incredible life she led. The last words I heard Mac say to me before I awakened suddenly were, "Don't worry, Jeff; I'll take care of him." I then sat up in bed quickly, with sweat on my brow. I mumbled to myself, "him"? I thought Mac was talking about Louise, but moments later Defender, who was sleeping at the foot of my bed, groaned once, licked my foot, and died.

I was heartbroken. Defender was only 11 years old, and although he had been lethargic of late, I never suspected he was near death. Then, as I put my covers over Defender and gave him one last kiss on his head, I now understood what Mac was trying to tell me. He was going to take care of Defender's soul. I felt better once I recalled the meaning of what Mac had told me. The link between the souls of the living and the guardians of our return had never been more evident.

My last case of major importance was the story of a man who believed he was a Maya seer. It was a fascinating case of a young man of forty who had had a massive stroke, and awoke a few months later from his coma. Suddenly, he was mentally transformed from a Mexican man who made a living blowing leaves around for a landscaping service to a high-ranking Maya priest from thousands of years ago. This was my kind of case.

I went to see him in his hospital room, and the man seemed to recognize me somehow. I understood his fast-paced Mayan lingo. I asked him who he was. He proudly said that as a child he had discovered cacao pods in the rain forest, and understood instinctively how to cultivate them. He went on to tell me that these football-sized and -shaped pods would ripen in six months, and he knew to ferment, dry and roast them. He taught his whole village how to do this, and they became the wealthiest village within fifty miles. The man had figured out how to make chocolate, and he became renowned for it. They even used cacao beans as currency. Only the wealthiest among them could afford this newfound delicacy.

I had a unique opportunity to ask a selfish question of this ancient Maya soul trapped inside a leaf-blowing Mexican from 1990. I had studied the Mayan calendar the last few years, and asked this man if he knew anything about how the calendar was created. He said that was not his specialty, but he knew general things. For example, he understood that the calendar was created about two-thousand years before he was born. He also said that the cycle ended on December 21, 2012. Because I had come back from the year 2133, rest assured this is not the end of the world, as some believe. This Maya soul did not think that this meant the end of the world either; more like the odometer on your car reaching 99,999 and then going back to zero, and then the cycles would begin again.

The Maya had help from the alien race known as the Zera in constructing the Mayan calendar five thousand years ago, which explains how the Maya knew so much about sunspot activity. I had had limited contact with the race known as the Zera to this point in my life. I met them a few times, but rarely spoke or exchanged thoughts with them. The Zera were the quiet race that sat silently as the Delp complained and the Rell exchanged thoughts with me.

CHAPTER 41

ARBITRATION

As I was about to leave the hospital room, the little Mexican man said to me, "The Zera need your help with something. Please go to the place you have seen them before as soon as possible." I was stunned by this request. Then the man drifted off to sleep. Moments later, he awoke as himself again; he was the Mexican leaf-blower, who wanted to go home to his wife and child. Even the effects of his stroke seemed minimized. Earlier in my life I would have been shocked by this consciousness transference, but I was getting used to these strange soul exchanges. It would seem that the Zera used this man as bait, so to speak, knowing I would get involved with his case. This man's Maya possession seemed to be a calling card for me to contact the Zera.

I called Clem, who was in one of Groom Lake facilities at the time, and I told him what had happened. Clem told me to come out and he would try to contact the Rell, who in turn would contact the Zera so we could get to the bottom of this. I may have been eighty-five years old, but I felt thirty-five in mind and body. These incidents that I kept getting myself involved in were clearly keeping me young.

When I arrived in Nevada, Clem had already gotten some answers for me. Through the Rell, Clem had found out that the Zera wanted me to help arbitrate a dispute with a fourth alien race I had never met. The Zera had chosen me for two reasons: they felt I was even-handed in my past dealings with them and, more importantly, they wanted me because of the gift the Defenders had given me, to understand all languages spoken in the Cosmos. The Zera felt that this made me the perfect galactic arbitrator.

The Zera and their opponent in this case, the Reckla, sent their representatives to Earth to argue the case in front of me. The case involved a corridor in space that both races claimed as their own. Again, I was no lawyer, but I knew the reasons I had been chosen to do this and I did my best. We were using the same clean room at Area 51 that we had in the past for these meetings. It was such a pleasure to not have to go through the mind-ripping headache process anymore. We spoke in verbal language and, thanks to the Defender, I understood every word spoken. Clem skipped this meeting. He was fearful of getting a stroke from the massive headache, and at our age, I didn't blame him. Clem trusted me to assess the situation and report back to him.

The corridor in question was between two galaxies. Each race had their own name for them, so to avoid confusion, and to simplify things, I called these galaxies One and Two. As it was explained to me, only one race could use a corridor at one time. There had been several accidents recently where ships were destroyed for using the corridor simultaneously. The Reckla had discovered the corridor a few thousand years before the Zera had, which obviously was in their favor. The Reckla, for reasons of their own, wanted this corridor kept secret from other races, and never filed the proper galactic paperwork.

I tried to put the case in my own mind in Earth terms. I viewed this as though the Reckla had found gold on a piece of land they were prospecting on, but never filed their claim with the authorities. The Zera found gold on the same land later on, and filed their papers properly. This was in essence the entire case. Neither side offered me much else to work with. I asked the Zera and the Reckla representatives a time ratio question, which became the key variable to my disposition of their case. I asked, "For one year of your lifetime, how many years would pass on Earth?" Due to the aliens living so much of their lives in a dimension outside of time, their answer was difficult for them to ascertain, but they rounded it off to around one hundred years.

Knowing that every hundred years of Earth time equaled approximately one year for the Zera and the Reckla let me use this ratio as a guide, and my resolution to this conflict was as follows: I told the Zera and the Reckla that they would have to share the corridor and alternate in one hundred Earth-year periods of time. I told the Zera that for the next one hundred Earth years, the Reckla were the only ones who could use the corridor between galaxies, and then one hundred years from the date of the ruling, only the Zera could use the corridor for the next one hundred years, and so on. Somehow, this simple ruling was sufficient for both sides.

My decision was not at all complicated, and neither race seemed to like or totally dislike what I had said, which I suppose is what makes an agreement possible. If one side feels that you ruled in the other side's favor, the chances of the agreement being adhered to are minimal at best. The Zera and Reckla did the equivalent of a handshake; they each touched the other's hip with their right hand. I had no idea the significance of this gesture, but it seemed to be the final acceptance of the ruling. Both races bowed their head to me in thanks and then vanished into thin air, as they crossed into their transdimensional realms.

I filled Clem in. He was happy that things worked out, and we soon returned to our normal lives again. My life was full spectrum: one day working on a galactic agreement and the next day watching reruns of "Sanford & Son." Now back in my lonely apartment, it was just me and the three geckoes once again. For no logical reason, I nicknamed the geckoes Mo, Larry and Curly.

Clem and I were not only close friends, but we shared the same physical problem. We each had an enlarged prostate gland. We would sit in my apartment playing cards while drinking pomegranate juice, eating avocados by dipping crackers into them, and then capping off the evening by taking the herb saw palmetto. Those three items seemed to keep our "butting" problems in check. I had actually learned about these three treatments for an enlarged prostate from my timeline. A top party official suffered from this ailment, so no expense was too great to find relief for him. I had read about these fruits and herbs in the medical newspaper from my timeline, and that the party leader's problem had abated.

CHAPTER 42
HILLMAN'S LAST REQUEST

Several unexciting years passed, and then I received a call from the Mossad in Israel that Hillman was dying and wanted to see me before his death. I had very mixed emotions about this. I was now well past eighty-five myself, and traveling for thirteen hours on a plane didn't appeal much to me, especially since I would be going to see someone I hated. But in the end I decided to go. I figured that Hillman had to be at least ninety-five years old, as he was at least several years older than me. The year was 1993. When I arrived in Israel they sent a car for me, which was a welcome surprise. I was driven to a private hospital where Israeli guards with machine guns stood at their posts. I assumed this was some sort of high-security hospital.

I was escorted by a guard to Hillman's room. Hillman must have lost 100 pounds; he actually looked older than ninety-five, which may be difficult for some to comprehend. Tubes in his nose and an IV drip in his arm, along with one of those fashion-statement hospital gowns, had reduced this once fierce and dangerous man to one you could almost have pity for. Hillman was dying of pancreatic cancer.

When Hillman noticed me, he did his best to sit up in bed, as if summoning his last ounce of strength to speak with me. "You made it. Thank you for coming," were his first words to me.

I pulled up a chair and told him, "You've looked better." Hillman smiled and told me I still had a quick wit. He asked

214

what I had been doing for the past thirty years. I considered telling him the truth, but realized there was no point. So I just answered him with "This and that," and then asked him what he had been doing.

Hillman then got his old swagger back a bit, and tried to tell me about his planting new Nazi seeds that were taking shape in today's world. Hillman had convinced himself history had not been changed at all. He believed that he was the beginning of the Fourth Reich, and the father of a new Nazi order. At this point I stood up and told Hillman to try and grasp the reality of the world today: The Nazi movement was all but dead. However, I soon realized that there was no use in trying to convince him of anything, as his mind was too rigid and jaded to hear the truth. As I moved to leave his room, Hillman said as loudly as his crippled body could muster, "Time will tell if my view of the future is correct."

I turned in the doorway, and my last words to Hillman on this Earth were, "I do know one thing, Hillman: be prepared to come back as a snake for your next 1,000 lifetimes, before you finally advance to the cockroach stage." Of course he had no idea what I was saying, which actually made me feel rather good. I was about to give Hillman a real piece of my mind regarding the cowardice of Nazis and how they prey only on the weak, but again, I stopped myself because I knew my words would not penetrate his twisted mind.

I left Hillman's room and was driven to the airport by a Mossad agent who surprised me with his inside information. "So aliens came to Earth to wager on dinosaur fights?"

Rather than play dumb or deny what the driver said, I responded, "That is the rumor." Clem had once told me that intelligence agents were a community unto themselves, and that it was difficult to keep secrets from one another. In this case, I assumed the davening rabbi was the Israeli source, but I had no way to confirm that. The rest of the ride was silent, except for the moment when I got out of the car and the Mossad agent said that Hillman would be dead in a week or two.

On the flight home I couldn't decide if this trip had been a complete waste of time or not. I did get a level of satisfaction from telling Hillman that he'd be coming back as a snake for 1,000 lifetimes, so the trip wasn't a total waste. I was tired. Suddenly my energy levels were down, and even my daily routine became more difficult. Making dinner for myself or going out each night for supper alone were my two unsatisfying choices. So, I decided to give the apartment to Victoria for whenever she came to New York. Victoria made a generous offer for me to live with her in London, which I did consider, but in the end I didn't want to burden her. Clem too invited me to stay with him and his wife, but as tempting as this offer was, Clem's wife was too loud, so that possibility lost its luster. So I decided to move to an assisted living facility, and you know the rest.

Jeff was worn out from telling his two-day-long story, so I drove him back to his room in the Queens Hilton. Jeff made me promise, once again, not to tell anyone what he had told me until at least ten years after his death, which I did agree to. Jeff seemed happier as he walked the halls and spoke to other inmates in our asylum, perhaps because he was able to share his tale with me. At least, that is what I told myself.

EPILOGUE

One day, an old, short, stocky man came to visit Jeff. From Jeff's description, it had to be Clem Rizzoli. I was dying to introduce myself, so I walked by Jeff's open door three or four times in a row, walking back and forth until he noticed me. When Jeff invited me into his room, I was introduced as "the caretaker of this facility."

Clem used this opportunity to hit me with a litany of complaints. "This place smells like death wrapped in mold and three-day-old fish. Do something about that!" I just smiled. I felt like I knew Clem intimately, though he didn't know it at the time. Clem wasn't done with me yet, as he bellowed, "Wipe that stupid smile off your face, and get to work improving the conditions around here."

Jeff then told Clem that he had told me everything. Clem was surprised at Jeff's admission, and then he turned to me and said, "Kid, if you mention one word of this to anyone else . . . ."

I cut Clem off before he was about to give me the details of my demise, and told him, "I made a promise to Jeff that I intend to keep. I won't talk. You two men have done so much to save the world and improve life that I am just in awe to be in your presence."

Clem looked at Jeff, shook his head and muttered, "Kid, will you get your head out from our asses long enough to get us something decent to eat?"

I got the message and left the room in search of lunch for them. When I returned, I heard Clem begging Jeff to come home with him and get out of this shit hole.

Jeff refused Clem's offer, but Clem returned once a week after that to visit. Jeff allowed me to bring a tape recorder to ask him questions from time to time. Anytime that Jeff was willing to talk with me, about any subject, I was there ready to listen.

Jeff was rarely eager to talk to me, but some days he did put up with a few questions. Jeff spoke of the voice in people's heads, or their conscience, being one of the jobs in the afterlife, or at least that was Mac's opinion. Mac believed that this was what determined if a soul was good or evil. If you had an evil advisor in your head, telling you to do dangerous or unlawful things, or if you had a more angelic voice in your head, might determine your future.

The ending of this book may seem more like a *Playboy* interview, but I did want to share what Jeff had shared with me before he died in 1999.

Q. What is your favorite television show?
A. *The Simpsons*. So very American
Q. Favorite movie?
A. *Dr. Strangelove*. It's not easy to make a comedy about the end of the world.
Q. What do you think the greatest dangers are to this time-line you helped create?
A. Nuclear proliferation, overpopulation, demographic shift.
Q. What would be your guess as to what life on Earth will look like in 100 years?
A. Sorry, far too many variables to venture an educated guess on that one.

Q. Do you believe in Heaven and Hell?
A. They certainly exist here on Earth. I grew up in hell. This timeline seems more balanced between the two.
Q. Who were the greatest Earth men you ever met?
A. That is a ridiculous question, but Churchill and Einstein impressed me.
Q. Do you have any regrets?
A. Not finding cures for the diseases that kill us all.
Q. Do you think the Defender will protect Earth from a major catastrophe?
A. Let's hope so.
Q. Do you believe in God?
A. The Defender's boss has to answer to someone. Yes.
Q. What advice would you give humans for the twenty-first century?
A. Live free, eat well, educate yourselves, control pollution of the air and water, and be good to your fellow man.
Q. If you could have one wish answered what would it be?
A. I'd like to know if my family from the alternate timeline would ever be born.
Q. What are your political leanings?
A. The left and right are both too extreme, stay in the center.
Q. Any ideas on how to make politicians better servers of the people?
A. Actually, I do have an opinion on that question. I believe that you must have at least five years of work in the private sector before entering politics. In this way you know what it's like to be the payer of taxes versus the recipient of others' tax payments. It's only logical to see both sides of the issue even-handedly.
Q. Any final thoughts?
A. Actually, I never told Victoria everything. I suppose that when you tell this story at some time in the future,

she will finally know the complete truth. That's a good thing. I view planet Earth as an apartment building. Each country owns an apartment in the building. Obviously, some apartments are larger than others. My point is that if someone starts a fire, there is a danger for all, so world peace must be the top priority.

In Jeff's last few years, he was the star in the assisted living facility. He settled arguments with Polish, Russian, Chinese, and Indian residents. He wasn't just an arbitrator for the Zera and the Reckla, but right here in Queens too.

Jeff died in his sleep in May 1999, with a large grin on his face. I wondered if Mac had told him a joke before he moved on. I called Clem and told him about Jeff's passing. He was understandably broken up. The funeral was scheduled for the next day, at a local church.

It was disappointing to me that such a great man had died, and there were less than ten people there to mourn him. Clem must have called Victoria, Mickey and Freddy. Louise's sister Pam came too. There were a few military-type people, and that was it. It was a typical funeral at the beginning, but Clem got fed up with the usual generalities that the priest was sermonizing all of us with, so Clem took to the stage. After pushing the priest aside, and telling him to sit down and "listen for a change," Clem gave a wonderful eulogy, with no written prepared remarks.

"Jeff was my best and only true friend for the past sixty years. I can't speak to everything that we were involved in over the years; actually, come to think of it, I can't tell you anything we did, but this guy lying here was special. He will never get the proper credit for his accomplishments in this life, but be darn sure he will in the next one." As Clem touched the coffin, he said, "See ya on the other side, pal."

Clem was followed to the podium by Victoria, who spoke in loving terms and left the stage in tears. Mickey consoled her as she moved offstage, and it looked to me like Jeff's death might have brought them back together, which I think would have made Jeff happy. We all then made our way in small procession to the cemetery. The service was quick, and I think Clem had frightened the priest into the Evelyn Wood version of the graveside service.

After Jeff's casket was lowered into the ground, and everyone else began to walk away from the grave, Clem and I saw something amazing. Before the workers at the cemetery began to shovel dirt onto the casket, a black dog wearing a red bandana, and carrying a white rose in his mouth, walked slowly to the open grave and dropped the white rose onto Jeff's casket. The dog stood there for a moment, and then walked off in the direction he came from.

I looked at Clem and he looked at me. No one else except the gravediggers saw this; I turned to Clem and whispered, "Was that?"

"Yeah, had to be." I walked arm in arm with Clem to help hold him up as we left the cemetery. Clem said to me as we were leaving, "Don't talk or write about any of this for ten years. The world needs a little more time." I made the same promise to Clem as I had made to Jeff.

Clem died two years later, and was cremated. It was the end of the beginning for all of us.